08/89

Cookson, Catherine.

oks   Bill Bailey's daughter / Catherine Cookson. --
London ; Toronto : Bantam, 1988.
   220 p.

03673669   ISBN:0593014316

I. Title

BILL BAILEY'S DAUGHTER

Other Books by Catherine Cookson

NOVELS

Kate Hannigan	The Mallen Girl
The Fifteen Streets	The Mallen Litter
Colour Blind	The Invisible Cord
Maggie Rowan	The Gambling Man
Rooney	The Tide of Life
The Menagerie	The Girl
Slinky Jane	The Man who Cried
Fanny McBride	The Cinder Path
The Garment	Tilly Trotter
Fenwick Houses	Tilly Trotter Wed
The Blind Miller	Tilly Trotter Widowed
Hannah Massey	The Whip
The Long Corridor	Hamilton
The Unbaited Trap	The Black Velvet Gown
Katie Mulholland	Goodbye Hamilton
The Round Tower	A Dinner of Herbs
The Nice Bloke	Harold
The Glass Virgin	The Moth
The Invitation	Bill Bailey
The Dwelling Place	The Parson's Daughter
Feathers in the Fire	Bill Bailey's Lot
The Mallen Streak	The Cultured Handmaiden

THE MARY ANN STORIES

A Grand Man	Life and Mary Ann
The Lord and Mary Ann	Marriage and Mary Ann
The Devil and Mary Ann	Mary Ann's Angels
Love and Mary Ann	Mary Ann and Bill

FOR CHILDREN

Matty Doolin	Mrs Flannagan's Trumpet
Joe and the Gladiator	Go Tell It To Mrs Golightly
The Nipper	Lanky Jones
Blue Baccy	Nancy Nutall and the Mongrel
Our John Willie	

AUTOBIOGRAPHY

Our Kate	Catherine Cookson Country
Let Me Make Myself Plain	

BY CATHERINE COOKSON AS CATHERINE MARCHANT

House of Men	Miss Martha Mary Crawford
The Fen Tiger	The Slow Awakening
Heritage of Folly	The Iron Façade

CATHERINE COOKSON

BILL BAILEY'S DAUGHTER

BANTAM PRESS

LONDON · NEW YORK · TORONTO · SYDNEY · AUCKLAND

TRANSWORLD PUBLISHERS LTD
61–63 Uxbridge Road, London W5 5SA

TRANSWORLD PUBLISHERS (AUSTRALIA) PTY LTD
15–23 Helles Avenue, Moorebank NSW 2170

TRANSWORLD PUBLISHERS (NZ) LTD
Cnr Moselle and Waipareira Aves,
Henderson, Auckland

Published 1988 by Bantam Press,
a division of Transworld Publishers Ltd
Copyright © Catherine Cookson 1988

British Library Cataloguing in Publication Data

Cookson, Catherine, 1906–
Bill Bailey's daughter.
I. Title
823'.914[F]

ISBN 0-593-01431-6

Printed in Great Britain by
Mackays of Chatham plc, Chatham, Kent
Photoset by Rowland Phototypesetting Ltd
Bury St Edmunds, Suffolk

PART ONE

THE BIRTH

1

'It's my turn to listen.' The six-year-old Mamie pushed Willie, her adoptive brother, to one side and he returned the gesture with more force as he said, 'It's always your turn; you've always got to be first.'

'Stop it! Both of you.' Fiona Bailey hitched herself up on the couch and, looking from her adopted daughter to her youngest son, said, 'I'm tired of you two squabbling. What's the matter with you these days?' She looked at the round-faced, curly-haired child whom she had spoilt somewhat more than her own children because of the circumstances under which she had come into the house. Her father had been one of Bill's men, a lad he had trained himself in the building business and in whom he had taken a most fatherly interest, seeing in the boy a replica of himself when young. And when a car accident had wiped out the little family with the exception of Mamie, who was then three years old, he was devastated; more so when the child's grandparents showed no intention of taking on the responsibility of their granddaughter.

It was the child herself who now brought her grandparents into the picture after answering Fiona's question with, 'He's always nasty to me.' Then turning on Willie, she cried,

7

'When I next go to see my grandma and grandpa I won't come back.'

'Good job too. Anyway, you cried to come back last time. Dad had to go and fetch you. You were howling your eyes out.'

'Willie! Oh dear me.' Fiona lay back on the cushions and put her hand to her head, saying, 'I used to have a nice family at one time. And I don't know what this baby will think when it comes.' She put a hand on the high mound of her stomach; then she turned her head quickly as her nine-year-old son remarked nonchalantly, 'It won't be able to think for a long time, years and years.'

The mother and son exchanged a long glance, and when she answered the twinkle in her son's eye by saying, 'Who knows? It might be a genius: start composing at three like Mozart, or it might be a great sculptor or an artist.'

'Some hope.'

'Willie!'

'Well' – Willie tossed his head from side to side – 'neither Mark, Katie, or me, and certainly not her' – he thumbed towards Mamie – 'show any signs of genius.'

'Well I never! We'll have to wait till Mark and Katie come from school and inform them that they're wasting their time studying because their brother thinks I have a family of numskulls.'

When the sitting-room door opened Fiona called across the room to her friend Nell who, two years ago, had come to live next door as Mrs Paget but was now married to Bert Ormesby, one of Bill's men, and for the first time in her life was really happy. 'You know what you're looking after, Nell?' she cried.

'Well, sometimes I wonder, but you tell me.'

'A bunch of near idiots.'

'Oh, I'm not surprised at that. I've thought that meself for a long time. Of course, some are worse than others. But how has this been revealed to you?'

'Oh, by my son here.'

8

'Well, Willie should know.' And she turned to him, saying, 'Your second lieutenant, Mr Samuel Love, is in the kitchen awaiting your presence.'

Almost before she had finished speaking Mamie had turned and made to run from the room, only to be stopped by Nell's arm.

'Leave go! Nell. I . . . I want to see Sammy.'

'Well, I don't think he wants to see you, my dear. As usual he's come to see Willie.'

'He does want to see me, he's my boy-friend.'

'Oh, in that case.' Nell removed her arm, and when Mamie darted from the room Willie turned and regarded his mother with a most pained look on his face, and Fiona said softly, 'Don't worry, dear. You know Sammy, he doesn't like girls.'

'She'll make him like her.'

'No, she won't. I mean, she won't be able to.'

'Why?'

'Well, if ever there was a he-boy, he's a he-boy, isn't he? Go on. Tell her to come back here, I want to see her; then take Sammy upstairs to the playroom.'

'Can he stay to tea?'

'Does he ever not stay to tea?'

Her son made a face at her; then hurried from the room. And Nell, walking towards the couch, said, 'The eternal triangle. How goes it?'

'The same as yesterday, dear, and the day before that. The only thing is I feel I'm going to explode. Did you ever see anything like it?' She again put her hand on her stomach. 'Can you remember? Was I ever slim? as flat as a pancake? You know, Nell, not one of the others was this size. If I hadn't been assured there's only one there, I would swear it's triplets, or more. When I was carrying the others they were hardly noticeable.'

'Well, you must remember they had a different father; this one owes its existence to Wild Bill Hickok.'

9

Fiona laughed. It was a quiet, contented laugh. She laid her head back on the cushion and, looking up at Nell, said, 'I don't think I've ever been so happy in my life. It's odd. I've felt well all the time I've been carrying. But not only that, I've had this feeling of contentment. Well' – she now nodded her head – 'I shouldn't say all the time because you know what happened when I was two and a half months. My goodness! will we ever forget that? You can't imagine, looking back, that anyone could kidnap Bill, could you, and practically murder him? And he's here now, thanks only to that little rough scrap in the kitchen there, Sammy Love, the child I hated on sight and went on hating, I'm afraid, until he saved Bill's life, all through his frequenting that filthy tip in order to pick up bits and pieces.'

'Oh, he wasn't on that tip that night to pick up bits and pieces, it was, as you know, to look for a milk jug or sugar basin to go with the broken silver-plated teapot he had found there and presented to you' – she was pointing towards the cabinet – 'and which still holds pride of place there.'

Nell sat down by the side of the couch and looked about the room musingly before she said, 'Life's odd, isn't it? The more you think about it the odder it becomes. Who would have thought that I'd ever marry Bert and be so happy that I'm afraid?'

'Why are you afraid? What do you mean?'

'Well, that it can't last. After those thirteen years with Harry, I keep saying to myself every morning, when will he change? I mean, Bert. When will he grow indifferent? When will he walk out on me for somebody else and give her a baby that I longed for for years? And when will he say, "I want a divorce"?'

'Now stop thinking like that! What's the matter with you? Bert would never do any one of those things, you know he wouldn't.'

'Yes, I know.' Nell nodded her head now. 'Yes, I do

know, yet I can't help being afraid. When you've been made to feel worthless, it's really hard to take in the fact that someone thinks . . . well, you're wonderful.' She pushed her hand towards Fiona as she grinned widely, adding, 'He does, he thinks I'm wonderful.'

'So do I, Nell, in a different way, so do I, and I'm so grateful that I have you. I can't imagine what I would have done without you, especially during this time.'

'Oh, the big fellow would have gone out and hauled somebody in. You would have managed. By the way, how's his pains?' She laughed and Fiona replied with a chuckle, 'He had cramp in the night. He had to get up and stamp his feet on the floor.'

'He's having a bad time carrying.'

They both laughed out loud now. Then Fiona, becoming more serious, said, 'If I've had worries at all during this period they've been about him. I've picked the wrong time to become pregnant. It would have to be, wouldn't it, just as he's starting work on the estate.'

'But that's going well, isn't it? Bert says it was a brainwave of Bill's to put the eleven disciples' – she pulled a face – 'in charge of gangs. They're already vying with each other as to who can get the most work or the best work out of their lot. Bert says it's funny to hear them in the cabin. He calls the cabin the hen cree. One of them threw some water over him yesterday because he said they were like hens with their first brood. And yet, you know, he's just as bad with his lot. Anyway, what would you like to eat besides apples? You're getting no more apples today; there'll be pips sprouting in your ears.'

'I don't feel very hungry, Nell.'

'You must eat; you've got to feed it. By the way, have you decided on names?'

'Yes. If it's a boy it's going to be Samuel.'

'Samuel?'

'Yes. Sam . . . u . . . el. Because, as Bill says, if it wasn't

11

for the Samuel that I heard pounding up the stairs a moment ago he wouldn't be here today.'

'And if it's a girl?'

'Angela.'

'Angela. That's nice. Did he choose that?'

'Yes, it was his idea. Because, as he says, it'll be his first real child and it will be like an angel to him.'

'Well, well. The big fella being sentimental.'

'You don't know the half.'

'Oh.' They both turned towards the door as the footsteps came running across the hall. 'Here comes the lady of the house.'

Katie had put on inches during the year. Every time Fiona looked at her she saw herself as a girl of eleven, straight, slim, luxuriant brown hair, deep brown eyes with arched brows and a well-shaped mouth, wide but matching the face. She could not imagine, though, that her tongue could ever had been as caustic as her daughter's could be at times.

'Hello. Hasn't it come yet, Mam?' Katie grinned down on Fiona; then, with a swift movement, she put her ear down onto her mother's stomach, saying, 'How's the alarm clock?'

'Get out of the way.' Fiona laughingly pushed her upwards. 'I've had enough of that for one day.'

'The juniors have been at it?'

'Yes, the juniors have been at it.'

'Their lugs want scudding.'

'*Katie!*'

'Well, Dad says that.'

'He might, but it doesn't sound the same on your tongue.'

'Not ladylike, eh?'

'Certainly not ladylike, not even girl-like.'

'Where are they?'

'They're upstairs with Sammy.'

'Oh. Is he here again? I thought that when Sir Charles

let them have the posh bungalow near Gran's we'd seen the last of him. Why doesn't he bring his bed?'

'Katie!' Fiona was wagging her finger at her daughter now. 'I've told you. We owe a great deal to Sammy. Never forget that. I won't and your father won't. So remember, we are all together and doing well and only through Sammy.'

'I'm not allowed to forget it.'

'Why do you dislike him?'

'I don't dislike him, Nell. It's only that . . . well, there seems to be only Sammy in this house.'

She now turned a painful glance on her mother and Fiona said, 'Oh, Katie, you know that isn't true.'

'It is, Mam. And you know when Dad comes in, what does he say? "Has Sammy been round?" At one time he used to yell out, "Where's my gang?"'

'He still does.'

'Yes, but then he says, "Has Sammy been round?" His gang isn't sufficient for him now.'

'Come here, Katie.'

Slowly Katie went to her mother, and Fiona, hitching her heavy body to the side, pulled her daughter down onto the edge of the couch and, putting her arm around her shoulders, she said, 'Your dad cannot forget that if it wasn't for Sammy he would now be lying very deep in that frightful tip. And, you know, Sammy hasn't a real home.'

'Well, it's a nice bungalow. It's bound to be when it's in the same crescent as Grandma's.'

'But he hasn't a mother.'

Katie's mouth now went up at the corner and she turned her head half to the side before she said, 'Grandma's trying to sit that exam, isn't she, Mam?'

'Katie! What put that idea into your head?'

Fiona had lifted her gaze towards Nell as she turned away, aiming to supress her laughter, and now, looking back at her daughter, she said, 'Your grandmother is only trying to be kind.'

13

'That's a change, isn't it?'

'Katie, what's come over you?'

'Nothing, Mam, only you know she's set her cap on that big rough fella.'

'She hasn't.'

'Mam, please.' Katie pulled herself away from her mother's hold now, saying, 'I'm older than Mamie; I'm nearly twelve.'

'You're not nearly twelve, you're eleven.'

'All right, all right, but on my next birthday I'll be twelve. I'm not a child.'

'You are a child, Katie. You are still a child.'

'Mam, don't say that. I'll tell you something. Sue's mother talks to her about everything. *Everything*.'

'What do you mean by *everything*?'

'Well, you know, men and things.'

Fiona felt the colour rising from her neck to her forehead, and, her voice stiff now, she said, 'I've told you all that is necessary along those lines. You know you haven't got to speak to strange men.'

'Oh, that!'

When her daughter flounced round and made down the room Fiona shouted, 'Katie! Come here.'

But her daughter took no heed and marched out of the room.

Fiona brought her hands tightly together and held them on top of the mound of her stomach. Had she really said she had never felt so peaceful in her life before or so happy? Yes, she had said that because that's how she felt. But had happiness blinded her to what was going on under her nose with her daughter? With Willie? Even with Mamie? The only one of her family who remained the same was Mark. Sometimes she forgot that her elder son was not yet thirteen years old for both his conversation and concern seemed at times to be that of a young man. She wished he was home, or better still Bill, but it would be half-past six before he

14

arrived. But she should be thankful it was that early in the evening when he came home now, for during the summer months it had been nine o'clock and sometimes later. He'd had a fortnight's holiday after coming out of hospital; then he seemed to have spent the next three months on the site for this was his first really big concern and he was determined that, as far as it lay in his power, everything would go right. And up till now, except for small hitches mostly concerned with the weather, everything had gone according to plan.

But no matter what time he came home now, almost immediately after his meal he would go into the study and work until midnight. Sometimes she would sit quietly in a chair watching him; and only recently she had said to him, 'If the plans are all worked out in the beginning why must you keep going over them?'

And he had answered, 'Because you can always better somebody's idea of the best. And I've discovered, what can look all right on paper can appear a mess when set up in a room, particularly bathroom fittings. Oh, and a thousand and one other things.' And when she had asked, 'Doesn't McGilroy object if you alter his plans?' he had replied, 'Oh yes. But he can object as much as he likes; if a thing doesn't look right to me then it comes out. The second time that happened we began to see eye to eye. But I still feel I cannot and must not relax.'

'He seems a nice man,' she had said.

He had grinned at her as he replied, 'He's always nice to women. Which reminds me, have you had your caller today?' And to this she had answered, 'Oh, Bill.'

She could never understand how he had become jealous of Rupert, Sir Charles Kingdom's secretary.

After the near tragedy that happened to Bill she took it as an act of kindness that the young man should drop in when he happened to come into town. And Bill did too at first, until on two occasions he himself happened to pop in out of hours when on his way to a board meeting in Newcastle.

15

On the first he found her dispensing tea to Mr Meredith who had insisted he be called Rupert. And nor were his feelings softened when on the second occasion Rupert Meredith was accompanied by Sir Charles himself.

When later on that particular evening he had said, 'What's his game?' she had stood up full of indignation, then pushed out her stomach, saying, 'I'm alluring, aren't I?' And to this he had answered, 'Yes, and so is your condition to some blokes . . . .'

She now lay back and stared at the fire. She had two weeks to go before the child was due. If all went well she'd be in hospital a fortnight today. And she was longing for the fortnight to pass. But of course, it might happen beforehand or even after. But whatever time it came she could see herself – as she had pictured hundreds of times since first knowing she was pregnant – watching Bill holding his own child. Only she knew how much this child was going to mean to him. She could laugh at the memory of that incident, in this very room, when she told him that he was to be a father, and for a moment she had imagined that he was going to pass out. And he had just returned from hospital that day, and so he could easily have done just that.

Her thoughts were disturbed by the pounding steps running down the stairs, and then the sitting-room door being unceremoniously thrust open and Willie coming in, accompanied by his friend Sammy Love.

'Mam, Sammy can't stay to tea tonight.'

'Oh. Why? Why not, Sammy?'

'Aw, 'cos.' The round brown eyes and the pugnacious face were riveted on the mound of her stomach.

'Because what?'

'Well, me da says I've got to get in and get the tea ready like I used to do in the flat so's your ma won't come in and start messin' about.'

Fiona nipped on her lip to stop herself from smiling, and

she kept her voice level as she said, 'Does . . . does my mother make it her business to go in often?'

'Aye, she does. Well, she did when me da left the key in the gutter. She asked him to at first like, 'cos she said she wanted to tidy up for us. But now me da says we mustn't put her out, take advantage like. Is it still kicking?' He now pointed to the mound. And Fiona, after a slight gulp, said, 'Yes; yes, Sammy; it's still kicking.'

'Let him hear it, Mam, the bumpety-bump.'

'Oh no, of course not.' She looked from her son to the nine-year-old auburn, nearly red-haired boy, and, seeing the defensive look she had come to know so well during the time when she could barely stand the sight of him, she said, 'You . . . you wouldn't want to hear its heart beating, would you, Sammy?'

There was a pause before he answered, 'Aye, if it's all right with you.'

'Go on, put your head on it.' Willie pushed Sammy now, and Sammy, turning and looking at his friend and in his inimitable way, said, 'All right. All right, hold yer hand, don't rush me.'

He now took the two steps that separated him from the couch and Fiona; and when she held out her hand to him and he placed his in it he did not immediately bend his head forward towards her stomach but looked at her, his face unsmiling. Then, his head to one side, he slowly lowered it down onto the mound.

'Do you hear it?'

He did not answer Willie's excited enquiry but remained still for a moment before straightening up and, looking at Fiona, he said, 'Ta.'

'You heard it, Sammy? You heard its heart beating?' Willie's voice was full of excitement.

'Aye. Well, I heard a kind of knock, knock, knock. That would be it like?' He looked at Fiona, and she said, 'Yes, that would be it, Sammy.'

17

'I'll tell me da. He'd be pleased you let me listen to it.'

'Perhaps he'd want to come and hear it an' all.'

'Willie!'

'I was only kidding, Mam.'

'Well, don't kid about such things.'

'Me da's got a new suit.'

'Has he, Sammy? That's nice. What colour is it?'

'It's dark blue. He wore it when he went to Mass yesterday mornin'.'

'You went to Mass together?'

'Aye.'

'That's nice.'

'It won't be for long, much more I mean, the year'll soon be up he says.'

'What do you mean, Sammy? Your father's only going to Mass for a year?'

'Aye, that's what he says. He made a promise or somethin'. He said that's what he owed Him.'

'Owed who?'

'God.'

Fiona swallowed deeply. Why was it she always wanted to laugh whenever she met this child or his father. She could never see either of them altering. In the months the boy had attended the private school with Willie it had made little impression on him except for the fact that he no longer said ya, or fink, and of course she must admit that his use of strong language had become a little less frequent, only when very excited or angry did he resort to colourful adjectives.

'Me da's goin' to get a car an' all.'

'Is he? Oh, that'll be nice for you both.'

'I don't know so much. I won't be able to drive until I'm seventeen, and then I'll be old.'

'No, you won't be old at seventeen, you'll just be a young man.'

'Aye; I know, but I don't want to be a young man.'

18

'Why?' Fiona's question was in earnest. And the answer come back in earnest. ''Cos then you think about lasses an' you get married an' they leave you. Then your troubles start.'

'Oh, Sammy.' She put her hand out again and caught his, and as she did so she thought, It's true: your early environment never leaves you. Her own never had. That's why she could never love her mother, because her mother never loved her. She put out her other hand and brought her son to her side too and, looking from one to the other, she said, 'When you are both seventeen you will be a pair of rips and you'll both have cars, racing ones. And the only trouble that'll happen to either of you won't come from girls or lasses' – she nodded her head, laughing now into Sammy's face – 'but from the police for speeding.'

Willie's laugh rang out at this, but Sammy only grinned and said, 'Mine'll be white like the Pink Panther's.'

'Mine'll be red.' Willie did a zoom over his mother's head with a twisting hand. But he stopped suddenly when Sammy cried, 'Don't do that! You'll frighten it.'

Both Fiona and Willie now looked at Sammy, who said, 'Well, you can. I mean, it was on the telly, t'other night. Some sheep were chased by a dog and they dropped their lambs afore time and the farmer said they were just like humans: give them a shock an' things went wrong.'

'Oh, Sammy.' Fiona now swung her leg slowly from the couch and, pulling herself upwards, she said, 'It would have to be a big fright before a baby dropped out. But thank you for being so protective.'

As she made her way slowly down the room towards the door, one hand on a shoulder of each boy, she said, 'Have you ever thought about getting a dog, Sammy?'

'Aye. Me da and me had a row about it just last week. He said I wouldn't look after it and it would be thrown out and I said, it wouldn't. But he said, it was cruel to leave a dog in the house all day, an' that's what would happen to it. Anyway, he said, it would mess the place up.'

'Well you could come home at dinner-time and let it out. I'll get Mr B to have a talk with your dad. How's that?'

He looked up into her face in that odd way he had of holding her gaze, then he said, 'Ta.' And again, 'Ta.'

'Miss Slater said you had to say, thank you, remember?'

'Aw.' Sammy pushed Willie none too gently, saying, 'Don't you start. I'll say ta when I like and thank you when I like, so that's that. I'm goin' now 'cos me da won't say ta when his tea's not ready.' There was a quirk to his lips now as he glanced at Fiona before pulling open the front door and running down the path, crying as he did so, 'Ta-ra! Ta-ra!'

After Willie shouted a similar goodbye, Fiona said as she closed the door, 'As Sammy has just said, don't start that. No more ta-ra's.' And as he ran from her, making for the stairs, she called after him, 'Do you hear?'

He was already half-way up them when he turned and grinned down at her, shouting, 'So long! Mam. So long.' And she went into the kitchen saying, 'So long! Mam. So long!'

'What's that?'

'That, Nell, is the result of checking my son from shouting ta-ra! after Sammy.'

'I like the sound of ta-ra!'

'You might, but I don't think it's in the curriculum at school. Sammy apparently was pulled up today for ta instead of thanks.'

'Oh, my, my! How dreadful!' Nell gave a short laugh as she nodded towards Fiona. 'You set that school a task when you got them to take Samuel Love.'

'Oh, that wasn't hard at the time; he was the town's hero, don't forget that. He could have got into Newcastle University at that time and they would have pinned a degree on him.'

They both laughed now; then Nell said, 'Get off your feet and sit down.'

20

'I've got to move, Nell; it's part of the exercise.'

'There'll be plenty time for you moving when you get rid of that. I've never seen anybody so big. It looks as if you're carrying a young elephant or a whale.'

'More likely a whale. It'll be three parts water.'

'Oh, here's the last of the tribe coming.' Nell looked down towards the back gate. Then she added, 'He seems to be the only one of them that doesn't run.'

Fiona joined Nell at the window, and she said, 'He's always walked like that, straight, steady. It's like his character.'

'Well, I'm glad there's one of them that's straight and steady. But here's one that'll have to run' – she turned from the window – 'if I don't want Mr Bertram Ormesby to arrive home to a plain table. Everything's set in the dining-room; and mind, see that the squad clears away.' She nodded towards Fiona. 'Anyway, I've been up there and I've told madam what she's got to do. And so, leave it to them, and no more interfering from you and standing at the sink till all hours. Hello there, Mark.'

'Hello, Nell. Boy! it's cold. Hello, Mam.'

When he leant forward to plant a kiss on the side of his mother's face he made no remark, such as Willie might have done, saying, 'I'll soon have to get a ladder,' or some such, but quietly asked 'How are you feeling?'

'Fine, fine; the same as I did when you went out this morning. How are you feeling?'

'Fine, fine; the same as I did when I went out this morning.'

They laughed together; then, looking to where Nell was getting into her coat, he said, 'Anything filling before tea, Nell? I'm starving.'

'Yes, there's plenty of dry bread and pullet.'

'Oh, that'll be nice.'

'Well, you know the new arrangement: help yourself to a snack until your dad comes in; then in the bottom of the

21

oven there's a shepherd's pie big enough to feed five thousand, and there's an apple pie to go with the custard I hope Katie is going to make.'

'She'll not.' Fiona flapped her hand towards Nell. 'I've had some of Katie's custard. Look, get yourself away and let me have my kitchen to myself for five minutes.'

'That's gratitude if you like.'

'Drive carefully; it's the peak hour.'

'And you be careful. . . .Ta-ra!'

As she went out laughing, Mark said, 'What was that last about; she generally says, bye-bye.'

'Oh, I was telling her about Willie and having to chastise him about ta-ra.'

'Oh.' Mark pursed his lips now. 'I shouldn't trouble. I bet before he's finished he'll end up talking like Sammy does now, and Sammy will be talking plain, unvarnished English.'

'I'm sorry, I can't agree with you, Mark, at least about Sammy. My fear is we'll have two Sammys. Anyway, everything all right with you?'

'Yes. . . .Mam.'

'Yes, what is it?'

'Roland's going skiing in February. There's a party from the school going to Switzerland. There's . . . there's still a vacant place and he wonders if . . . well, if I could go. But . . . but it costs a lot of money.'

'Skiing? Would you like to go?'

'Oh, yes, Mam. Oh, yes, I'd love it. But as I said . . . it costs. . . .'

'How much?'

'. . .'Over two hundred pounds.'

'Over two hundred. It is a lot of money.' She stretched her upper lip as she nodded at him. 'Well, we'll have to ask your dad, won't we?'

'Yes; yes, we'll have to ask him. But it's not only that; there'll be clothes, you know. You can hire the skis and

22

the boots, Roland says, but . . . well, there's other things.'

She put her arm around his shoulder, saying, 'Don't worry about that. When your dad comes in let him have his bath and his meal, then we'll get at him.'

'You're for it then, Mam?'

'Wholeheartedly. And I shouldn't be a bit surprised but I'll come with you.'

He leant his head against her shoulder, and when she asked, 'What did you say there?' he looked at her through blinking eyelids and said, 'Nothing, nothing. I'll . . . I'll take my snack upstairs.' He went to the fridge, and after opening the door he asked, 'Is this mine on the plate?'

'Yes. And if you get all that down you, you won't have any room for dinner.'

She watched him close the fridge door, then go out of the kitchen without looking towards her again. And she stood where she was for a time, her hands joined on top of her bulging stomach.

Her son had said to her, 'You're wonderful.'

She was so lucky.

She was crossing the hall when the front door bell rang.

She was surprised to see her mother. Mrs Vidler phoned practically every day, but her visits were few and far between.

'Oh! this cold.' The elderly woman bustled into the hall. 'The wind goes right through you. No, no, dear, I'm not staying; I've just come . . . well, I want a word with you. Are we alone? I mean. . . .'

'Yes, yes; they're all upstairs.'

Mrs Vidler hurried into the sitting-room. Fiona followed, more slowly, and when they were seated, she said, 'Is . . . is anything wrong?'

There was nearly always something wrong when her mother phoned; there was always something wrong when she visited her. She had been very sympathetic when she

23

thought that Bill was dead, but on his recovery she had reverted to her natural self; and yet not quite, because of her new interest in Davey Love and the boy. Of course, this interest could have been put down to motherly feelings, but she, knowing her mother, was well aware that she held no motherly feelings towards the big raw good-looking Irishman which in a way filled her with pity. She was well aware of her mother's need of a man, but why she should pick on this raw, uneducated yet good-hearted and amusing invidivual, she would never know because refinement was her second name.

'I'm going away for a while, dear.'

'Going away?'

'Yes, that's what I said, going away, and for perhaps a month.'

'A month?'

'My dear, stop repeating my words. I said, I'm going away for perhaps a month. Is it unusual that one should take a holiday?'

'Where are you going for perhaps a month?'

Not immediately, but after a pause, her mother said, 'America.'

'*America?*'

'Yes; you've heard of it, haven't you?'

'Mother, please don't be facetious. Why has this come about all of a sudden? Who's going with you?'

'There's no one going with me, dear. And it hasn't come about all of a sudden. I've been thinking about it and preparing for it for some weeks.'

'But there must be a reason. America, of all places. And . . . and on your own, and. . . .'

She watched her mother rear now: the old defensive look came back on her face and her voice was stiff as she said, 'Don't say that, Fiona . . . at your age. I am merely turned fifty. I'm not dead yet.'

Turned fifty? Her mother was fifty-eight, if she remembered rightly. Of course, she must admit she didn't look it, except there were those bags under her eyes and lines running from the corner of her mouth and marking her upper lip. Yet her bone structure was good; her high cheek bones stopped the cheeks from sagging. Yes, she could pass for fifty, or a little less, when she was made up, as she was at present. But why this trip to America? She said, 'Do you know anyone there?'

'Yes. Yes, I have been corresponding with someone there for some time now. And don't look surprised, Fiona. You see I have my own life to lead. You definitely have yours and haven't paid much attention to me or my doings. Oh. Oh' – she held up her hand now – 'I'm not blaming you. In your present condition I know how you must be feeling, but there were times when you weren't in your present condition and you must admit that then you didn't feel for me, or ask if I was lonely. . . .'

'Mother! You have been surrounded by your women' – she'd almost said cronies – 'friends for years: bridge friends, coffee friends, church friends; there's hardly a week goes by that you don't take a trip with them.' She could have added, 'And during the years that I was lonely and struggling to bring up three small children you only came here when it suited you, and then it was nearly always to interfere and cause an upheaval about one thing or another.' She sighed now as she said, 'Well, all I can say, Mother, is I hope you have a wonderful time.'

'There's no doubt about that, I'm sure I shall.' She was about to turn towards the door when she hesitated, then looked back at Fiona and said, 'By the way, did you tell Mr . . . Love that you thought it was too much for me to pop in and see to their meals?'

'No, I certainly did not; in fact, I have never discussed you with *Mr* Love.' And she emphasised the mister.

'Well, that is something in your favour. Now I must be going.'

25

'When are you leaving for America?'

'The day after tomorrow.'

'*So soon?*'

'No, it isn't so soon. I told you the arrangements have been going on for some time. Anyway, I may not see you again before I go, but I do hope everything goes well with you at your confinement.'

They stood facing each other at the front door now, and as Fiona looked at her mother she thought: Mother and daughter, and there was the mother saying, 'I'm going off to America for a month. I hope everything goes well with your confinement.' But she had never been an ordinary mother. She recalled the day after Mark was born when her mother stood by the bedside and said, 'Make a firm stand. Don't let this happen again.' And when she had said, 'Have you seen the baby?' Her mother had answered, 'All babies look alike at this age.'

That empty place somewhere below her ribs opened its door again and for a moment she felt she was about to cry. But why should she? She had everything: a loving family and an adoring man. So why should the lack of mother love be an empty space inside her?

'Goodbye, dear.'

'Goodbye, Mother.'

'Aren't you going to wish me a safe journey and a happy holiday?'

'Yes; I wish you both, Mother.'

Mrs Vidler stared at her daughter, then said, 'You were always so enthusiastic over my doings, weren't you, dear?' And then leaned forward for the maternal kiss, and without further words pulled open the door and went out.

Fiona had switched on the outside light, but as she watched the prim figure walking away she called, 'How are you going to get home, Mother?' One heard of old ladies and young ones too being attacked in the streets in the dark, and the Crescent was situated almost half a mile away. But

26

she needn't have worried because Mrs Vidler turned and said, 'I do have a taxi waiting, dear.'

Of course, she would have a taxi waiting; her mother always looked after number one. But taxis were expensive, as were trips to America, and she was always putting it over that she could just manage to exist in the middle-class way she had been accustomed to all her life.

'Mam.'

She looked up to where Katie was making her way down the stairs, two at a time as usual.

'That was Gran, wasn't it?'

'Yes; yes, that was Gran.'

'Has she upset you?'

'No, no dear. Would Gran ever upset anyone?' She pulled a face at her daughter and Katie said, 'Would there ever be a time when she didn't? Come on and sit down.' She took her mother's arm as if to give her support and escorted her back to the sitting-room, and to the couch. And when, having sat down by her mother's side, she did not begin to chatter by asking a question or expressing her adverse opinion of something or someone, Fiona said, 'Anything wrong?'

'Mam.'

'Yes?'

'Can I ask you something, personal like?'

'Yes, of course, dear.'

There was a long pause before Katie, looking into her mother's face, said, 'Do you love me?'

Fiona drew her head back as if to get her daughter into focus, and then she said, 'What a question to ask, Katie! Of course I love you. You know I love you. I . . . I love all of you.'

'That's it.'

'What do you mean, that's it?'

'That's what Sue said her mother said: she loved them all, the six of them, en masse. That's what Sue said, they

27

were loved en masse because there wasn't time to love them singly. Sue said you got advice doled out to you singly, but the other . . . well, it was in a lump.'

'Katie' – Fiona took her daughter's hands and held them tightly between her own – 'you're an individual. You are my daughter and I love you for yourself.'

'Do you love Mark and Willie like that too?'

Fiona paused before she answered this, and then she said, 'Yes. Yes, in a way. I love you each for yourself, not en masse.'

'What about Mamie?'

'Well' – Fiona again paused – 'Mamie comes into a different category. It was compassion I felt for Mamie first. But now I love her too. You understand? You understand me?'

'Yes. Yes, I do, Mam. But as Sue says, it'll be different when that comes.' She now poked her finger gently into the mound of Fiona's stomach. 'She says it was like that in their house because there was nine years between the last one and the new one, and the new one is now three years old and Sue says life has never been the same since it came.'

Fiona didn't speak for almost a full minute, but continued to look at her daughter. But she wanted to, she had wanted to say immediately, 'That Sue says too much; and I don't like your being friends with her. She's a year older than you in age, but apparently much older in her ideas, which she doesn't hesitate to voice.' But what she forced herself to say was, 'No two families are alike, Katie. Ours is a very special family. And I can assure you when the baby is born you'll all love it, and I shall continue to love you all . . . individually. Remember that. Individually.'

'Where's everybody?'

At the sound of the voice Katie jumped up from the couch, crying, 'That's Dad! He's early.'

As she went to pull the sitting-room door open Bill pushed

28

it from the other side, saying, 'Now Lady Bailey, are you pushing me out or welcoming me in?'

'You're early.'

'Is that a fault?'

'No, no; but it's only about half-past five.'

'I'll go back.' He took two steps backwards, and Katie, grabbing his hands, said, 'Do you want a cup of tea?'

'No, he doesn't,' said Fiona from the couch. 'We can have dinner any time now.'

'I want a cup of tea, madam.' He made one flapping movement with his hand towards her; then turning to Katie, said, 'Yes, hinny, a cup of tea, sweet and strong.'

'Aye, boss.'

'She seems in a happy mood.' He came quickly up the room now and, pushing Fiona's legs to the side, sat on the edge of the couch. Then turning his head sideways, he put his ear to her stomach, saying, 'Hurry up you! You've got me worried; you're comin' in between me and my work.' Lifting his head, he asked gently, 'How are you feelin', love?'

'Fine.'

'You know something? I'll have to stop calling you "love". Every time I say that word I think of Big Davey. How about pet?'

'No, I don't like pet, I'd still rather have "love", even with the image of Big Davey.'

'The house seemed quiet when I came in, no ructions from above.'

'Oh, you just missed those earlier on before Sammy went home. . . .I've got news for you.'

'Good or bad?'

'Well, it all depends upon how one sees another person. I think from your point of view it'll be good. Mother's going away for a month.'

'Oh, that is good. Where is she going?'

'America.'

'*What!*'

'That's what I said when she told me.'

'What's she goin' to do there?'

'Don't ask me. She says she's going for a holiday. She's been arranging it for a long time, she said.'

'She's up to something.'

'What can she be up to in America?'

'Your mother, my dear, never does anything without a purpose. You know that. Anyway, I know somebody who'll be glad she's out of his hair for a time, and that's Davey. I know all his little movements now, his reactions, and he's been tryin' to corner me for days. But I've had somebody with me or I've been on the site. You know, between you and me, I think it's indecent the way she's chased that fella. She's old enough to be his mother, she is really.'

'You needn't emphasise the fact, I know it too well. It's most embarrassing, especially since he stopped leaving the key handy for her. Why he did it in the first place was likely because he looked upon her as a motherly old soul.'

'What I can't understand' – and now Bill shook his head as he laughed – 'is that she's so stinkin' uppish, so refined, she's looked down her nose on me so much that she's cross-eyed, and yet, what does she do but set her cap at a fella like Davey Love who, let's face it, even from my point of view, is a pretty rough diamond. My! My! Well, I've never been able to fathom it.'

'Well, you should have, with your insight into the sexual activities of all mammals, especially the two-legged ones.'

'Aye well, that might be so, but goin' by her age there's nineteen years between them and that's indecent.'

Fiona half-cocked her head and said, 'Taking the argument a little further: it wouldn't be indecent if it was the other was around, the man nineteen years older than the woman, would it?'

'No. No, it wouldn't. That's nature. Anyway, it still

wouldn't have been so bad if she had picked on somebody of her own standard, at least what she considers her standard. Say now she had taken a shine to Rupert. Now there, he would, I should imagine, have been up her street, socially and in every other way. By the way, has he called in today?'

'No, he hasn't dear; and I'm so disappointed.'

'Watch your lug. You know, I could dislike that fella. He's everything I am not, and too, he's had a marvellous upbringing and a first-class education. But what is he doin' with it? Secretary to Sir Charles. And what does that mean? He is just a glorified chauffeur.'

'Oh, Bill, what's the matter with you? You used to like him. When you first got to know him you thought he was a splendid fellow.'

'Yes, perhaps; but I've changed me mind since he started visiting you, and knowin' that you more than like him.'

'I don't more than like him. You know something? I . . . I feel he's lonely.'

'Oh, my God!' As if he had been prodded with a fork, Bill rose from the couch. 'Don't take that tack. My! He has got to you.'

'*Bill.*' She brought her legs from the couch and, pushing herself upwards, she said, 'You've got to stop this. It . . . it upsets me that you should go on like this.' When her voice broke she was immediately in his arms and he was saying, 'Aw, love. I'm sorry. I am really. But I'm worried sick. I want to be with you all the time an' I've got to be on the job. And there I come in and he's sittin' an' you're natterin' away as happy as Larry. And it's at that time I should be happy for you. But let's face it, I suppose it's the old inferiority complex escaping.'

Fiona stared into his rugged face. Inferiority complex. That's the last thing anyone would imagine could be tacked on to this boisterous and, let her now face it, loud-mouthed individual. The man who had bragged he was the middle-of-the-road man where women were concerned; neither the

31

young nor the old were going to catch him. And this was true. He had only come to her as a lodger to escape the attentions of his middle-aged landlady. But what did one know really about the make-up of another, even as someone as close as he was to her? Inferiority complex. That was the first time she had heard him use that term; but being Bill, he knew himself better than anyone else did.

She now took his face between her hands and in a voice that was soft and full of caring, she said, 'Bill, there'll never be anyone in my life but you. Never. Even if you walked out tomorrow, no one could or would replace you. I love you as I never thought to love anyone in my life. In fact, I didn't know what love was until I met you. All I want in life is to make you happy.'

He said nothing; he just stared at her for a moment, then dropped his head onto her shoulder, and she held him close, as close as her stomach would allow.

'Here's your tea, sweet and strong . . . and stop necking.'

They drew apart, and he turned to Katie, saying, 'Thanks love. And . . . there'll never be another you. I heard that on the radio comin' over. It's a nice song. Suits you.'

'Flatterer. What do you want me to do? Get out and leave you two alone?' She looked at her mother and said, 'Mam, I think we had better have dinner because that shepherd's pie will soon need a crook to dig it out of the dish; from what I gathered when I opened the oven door it's going dry.'

'Well, call the rest, dear, we'll have it now. And you' – she pointed to Bill – 'don't blame me if you have indigestion after eating meat on top of tea. Come on,' she said, taking his hand now, 'give me a hand to carry in the dishes.'

'Carry in the dishes, she said,' said Katie, looking at Bill. 'She needs somebody to carry her in, doesn't she? What do you bet she doesn't go the full time.'

'Katie! please.'

'Your bet's on. I bet you . . . what?' Bill pursed his lips. 'Five quid that she goes to the very day.'

'*Five quid.*'

'Pounds, Katie.'

'All right, five quid, or five pounds, that's a lot of money. I'll have to take it out of my bank.'

'Well, are you on or off?'

'I'm on. And that means if it's before or after you pay me.'

'Aw! now you're stretching it. Before, you were willing to bet it would be before. Well what about it?'

'Meanie. All right, you're on. Mam.' She turned to Fiona. 'You put a spurt on; I can't afford to lose five pounds.'

'No dear; you can't; and with Christmas coming,' said Fiona as they went across the hall. And, looking at Bill, she added under her breath, 'Pity I didn't arrange things better. I could have given you a Christmas box then.'

Dinner was over; the children had washed up and were now upstairs in the playroom, and Bill was again settled behind his desk in the study and Fiona seated in the big leather chair to the side of the fire. She stopped her knitting when Bill stopped writing and looked at her, saying, 'I set four new ones on this mornin', and it amazes me that with all the unemployed in this town there aren't men queueing up for jobs. And of the four there was only one who really showed any interest. Apparently he had been a clerk and was in his late forties, but he said he had been on the dole for two and a half years and would be willing to try to turn his hand to anything. The other three seem to have been in and out of jobs like Yo-Yos. "Why did you leave your last job?" I asked one. "Well it was the travelling. You see, mister, I never got in until half-past six at night and by the time you have a meal and a wash it was practically the next mornin', and I had to leave at seven again. That was no life." God in heaven!'

'Yes, but how are things otherwise? I mean the schedule and so on.'

'Oh, the schedule. We seem to be a bit ahead. And the board seems well satisfied. We had a contingent round yesterday but some of them ask bloody silly questions though. What would be the saving if you could cut down on this, that, or the other? I answered one particular gentleman bluntly by saying, "inferior buildings". Another asked why we put lime with the cement. So you could pick the pointing out between the bricks with your fingers, I said to that one, and he believed me; I had to put him straight. Some blokes feel they must say something no matter how stupid. The fact is we've been through all this in the boardroom, minutely and minutely. . . .There's the bell. Who can this be at half-past eight? Your mother likely to say she's not going to America, or will I accompany her. Now sit where you are; I'll go and see who it is, that's if one of the squad doesn't get there first.'

None of the squad appeared in the hall, and when he opened the door it was to see Davey Love standing there.

'Hello, boss. I'm sorry to trouble you.'

Bill suppressed a sigh and said, 'Come in. Come in, Davey.'

'It's a cold night; cut the ears off you.'

'Yes, it is,' said Bill. 'We are in the study. There's a proper fire in there not artificial logs; come along.'

As they entered the study Bill said, 'Here's Davey, Fiona. He wants a word.'

'Oh, hello, Davey. Do sit down.'

'Ma'am, I feel I'm intrudin', but it's of necessity. You know what I mean?'

'Well, she will when you tell us why you're intruding. Sit down, man.'

Davey sat on a straight-backed chair, a hand on each knee, his cap dangling from one. He leant forward more towards Fiona than to Bill and said, ''Tis a delicate subject that I'm about to bring up, but I'm troubled. And knowin' me, it isn't often, you know, that I'd be lost for words, but

34

at this minute, as God's me judge, they're all stickin' in me gullet afraid to jump out an' into me mouth in case they upset you, ma'am . . . 'cos, you see, 'tis about your own ma I would speak.'

Fiona, resisting casting a glance in Bill's direction, said, 'Don't be afraid to speak about my mother, Mr Love.'

'Well, even with your permission, ma'am, I'm still chary of utterin' me thoughts. But afore I begin I'd like to stress this point. Aye, I would, an' it's this: me thoughts aren't made up of 'magination in this case; there's no Irish blarney coatin' the facts. The fact is, ma'am, that your ma . . . your mother has got the wrong end of the stick. Aw, begod! begod! how can I put it?'

'I'll put it for you, Davey. You mean she's been chasing you?'

Davey looked at Bill for a moment; then his gaze dropping away and his head swinging from side to side, he said, ''Tis a rough way to put it, boss, but that's the top an' bottom of it. And' – he raised his eyes now and looked at Fiona – 'I'm scared. I am. An' that's a strange thing to come from me lips, at least with regard to women, 'cos I've never been scared of a woman in me life. I get on with women, and I suppose that's the trouble in this case. But you see . . . well, how can I put it, ma'am, but I thought she was only bein' motherly. An' what man, I ask you, would say he didn't want a woman of her calibre to be motherly? 'Twas a nice feelin' at first: there was the table set all ready for the lad's tea, and mine an' all, when I come in. And there was me washin' sent out to the laundry. Begod!' He now slanted his gaze towards Bill adding, 'Don't those bug . . . I mean those laundry blokes, charge. You could get a new shirt for what you have to pay for their washin' an' ironin'. It must be the pins they stick in that put the price up.' He gave a small grin now. 'But, give the devil his due, I've never been so clean in me life afore. As for the youngster, he's become sick of the sight of soap, for she's had him washin' his hands

when he went to the lav. Well, 'tis only right, I suppose' –
he was nodding his head now – 'in that case. But afore his
tea and after his tea! She was even there at times in the
mornin', afore he went out to school, examinin' his nails.
It got that way that I hoped he'd give her a mouthful, you
know the way he used to an' that would've put her off. But
now I don't think it would have. She's a tenacious woman,
your ma.'

Fiona felt the child inside her wobble, and she had the
greatest desire to stop herself from bursting forth in high,
almost hysterical laughter. She blinked her eyelids a number
of times as she looked at the big raw Irishman now appealing
to her, saying, 'What am I goin' to do, ma'am?'

'Get yourself a woman. Bring one in.'

'Oh Bill!' Fiona shook her head.

'Never mind, oh Bill!' Bill was nodding at Davey now.
'That's what to do. Be cheerful about it. Introduce her to
Mrs Vidler. That'll knock the nail right on the head.'

'You know, boss, them were me very thoughts at times,
but, you see, the Crescent isn't the kind of place that you
do that kind of thing, is it? They're nearly all old dears an'
highly respectable people an' they've been very kind, I mean
. . . well, they've been very civil to me an' the lad. Of
course, it was all 'cos of the papers, you know, an' makin'
Sammy out to be a hero an' all that twaddle. They fell over
themselves at first; not so much now, you know; but still
they've been very civil. An' the type of woman that might
suit me mightn't suit them.'

'To hell with them! Just say that to yourself. It's your
life. And anyway, you're divorced, you could marry
again.'

'Aw begod! no. The fryin' pan put the fear of the fire into
me; I'm takin' nobody in on a permanent basis like. No,
sirree! 'cos you see I've got this bit of a temper. Well, I did
the nine months in Durham 'cos of it – didn't I now? – for
plasterin' me wife's fancy man's face all over the wall. No;

no more marriages. An' that's why, you see, that life appeared rosy when your ma took such an interest in us: I had a mother at last, I thought, not like the real one, an' the lad had a granny not like his real one.'

'Tell me' – Fiona leaned forward now – 'what's made you think otherwise then, that she doesn't still think of you as a mother?'

'Aw, ma'am. Ma'am. There's some things in this life you can't explain, not even God himself could put it into words. 'Tis the way some women have: the things they drop you know, little hints; an' the way they titivate themselves up. An' she could, couldn't she, your ma? Not that she looks her age. I've told her time an' again that nobody would take her for a day over forty.'

Bill's laugh was a deep guffaw, and he ran his hands through his hair. 'Aw, Davey Love, I thought you'd have more sense than that. Not a day over forty. You've asked for it. All you've got you've asked for. Anyway, she won't trouble you for the next few weeks, she's goin' to America.'

'She's goin' to . . .?'

'Yes.' Fiona now nodded towards him. 'She came in not so long ago to tell me that she's going on a holiday to America. And who knows? She might meet her soul-mate on the journey.'

'Praise be to God and His Holy Mother that she does. Praise be to God. Aw, you've lightened me day. You know what I was goin' to say next? That we must up an' leave, an' that would be a shame. I put it to the lad last night: I said, "We might have to leave here." "Why for?" he said. "Well, you don't want another ma," I said. "It depends," he said. "How about Mrs Vidler?" I said. "Bloody hell!" he said. Oh dear, 'tis sorry I am, ma'am, 'tis sorry. But he only uses language when he's troubled like. And he was troubled. Aye, begod! he was, 'cos you know what he said? "You might have to do it, Da," he said; 'cos if you didn't

37

you might upset Mrs B." You gave him leave to call you that, didn't you, ma'am, 'cos that's what he said, that I might have to take on your ma, 'cos I might upset you. 'Cos he has a great feelin' for you. Oh aye, past understandin' the feelin' he has for you. But it's good news, oh aye, 'tis good news, America.'

Bill had to make himself go down on his knees and poke the fire, then add more coal to it. And when, after dusting his hands, he sat back in his chair his face was red, not only from the flames. 'Now look here, Davey,' he said: 'take no notice whatever of the other occupants of the Crescent – they've all got their own dark secrets; there's not a house anywhere that hasn't – you find yourself a lass, a nice one for preference, not a beer slugger from the Dirty Duck. By the way, are you still goin' there and washin' up the glasses?'

'No, boss, no. Since I've been on this job I've hardly been in the place but twice. No, I left that when I left Bog's End, and me patronage now is given to the Crown.'

'Oh, the Crown. That's a nice pub, the Crown.'

'Aye, it is that. An' they get some nice folk in there an' all, all types, but all respectable.'

'Aye, yes indeed they do, at the Crown. If I remember rightly there's a nice barmaid in there, auburn-haired, good figure, name of Jinny.' He looked at Fiona now, and when he winked at her she said, 'We'll discuss her later, Mr Bailey.' And this brought a laugh from Davey, and he said, 'Don't think you need to worry, ma'am, not in that direction. But aye, she's a nice piece, that. I've had many a crack with her. And I know this about her: she's been divorced these two years back, an' no children. She lives with her brother up Melbourne Road.'

'Well now, what are you waitin' for? You'll lengthen those cracks if you've got any sense, boyo, and you'll have her installed by the time Mrs Vidler returns.'

'Aw, boss, that'd take a fast worker indeed, and I'm not

all that fast in that direction. Women never take me, what you call, seriously. They have a laugh at me; I'm good for a joke. Anyway, if I was for pickin' up with a woman an' Father Hankin got wind of it, begod! he'd expose me from the altar. He's hard on me heels now 'cos I told him quite plainly, that was in confession of course, that I was only goin' to Mass for a year to pay me debt to Him' – he now thumbed towards the ceiling – 'and once that's done, well, we're back where we started. You'd think those fellas, 'cos after all what are priests but men, well, you'd think now that they wouldn't remember what was said to them in confession, wouldn't you? They're not supposed to blow the gaff; but begod! they must have pockets all over their brains, and in one of 'em he's stored what I told him 'cos before that he didn't take any notice to me, I was just one of those thick Irish blokes that go to Mass 'cos they're frightened not to. They're all scared that they'll get knocked down an' die in mortal sin, 'cos they still believe in hell's flames. But there was this one' – he pointed to his chest – 'tellin' him the truth. And I tell you, since then me Guardian Angel couldn't be stickin' to me closer than he is.'

'Shut up, will you? Shut up! Come and have a drink.' Bill's cheeks were wet. 'And you stay there' – he now touched Fiona on her bowed head – 'and I'll bring you one in, non-intoxicant of course.'

Davey was on his feet now and bending towards Fiona, saying, 'Good-night to you, ma'am. I'm glad we've had this crack; I feel better now. And who knows: Things'll work out; they generally do. Oh aye, they generally do. And if I'm not to see you afore your delivery, ma'am, may the Holy Mother of God be with you on that day and help you through your trauma.'

'Come on away with you, will you? . . . Dear God in heaven! I'm talkin' as Irish as you.' Bill put out his arm and almost hauled Davey from the room, leaving Fiona to sit back in her chair with the tears running down her face. . . .And may the Holy Mother of God be with you on that day and help you through your trauma. Oh, Davey Love, Davey Love, and Sammy Love. How they had affected this family since they had come onto the horizon, and not least with laughter.

2

She had only another week to go, at least according to her.
But the betting in the house was varied. You could say a
book had been set up in the family Bailey. It had gone on
from Katie's betting Bill, to Katie's betting Willie; then
Willie's betting Mark, and Mark's betting Nell, and Nell's
betting Bill, the bets being kept in the book by Mark with
the amounts and dates of arrival against each case. Willie
stood the lowest, aiming to gain or lose only twenty pence.
Katie's bet still remained at the top of the list.

A lot of laughter had been caused by the *book*; but, a
certain amount of dissent too: on the one hand, Bill had
laughingly said, she had kept her family off drugs, drink and
smoking, only for them to take to gambling, and that, in
his mind, was much worse than drink; whilst on the other
it had heightened the war between Katie and Willie and
caused it to be inflamed still further by Mamie's preference
for Sammy. Where at one time she had adored Willie and
relished his impatience with her and had been given the
brush off every time she showed her affection for him, now
she almost infuriated him by not only ignoring him, but
also, in her childish yet knowing way, extolling the virtues
of Sammy Love. And if Samuel hadn't been wise enough

41

to abhor little girls, as he once did nuns, there would certainly have been a rift between him and Willie.

With regard to Sammy, Fiona had put her foot down: he was not to be brought into the *book*. It was bad enough her family betting on her. Yet Sammy's being excluded from joining the *book* was brought into the open at the tea-table.

The old routine of the children sitting down to tea when they returned from school had been resumed, for Bill was now much later home, and the children couldn't be kept waiting for a meal. So here they were, all sitting round the kitchen table, including Sammy.

Nell, who was about to leave, said to Fiona, who was pouring tea out, 'Now look, Fiona; leave that! Mark or Katie or any of them can surely pour tea out if they want more. Go and sit yourself down.'

'No, Mam, you stand up, walk about.' Katie was laughing up at Fiona. 'And you know why?'

'Katie, stop it!' But Fiona shouldn't have glanced from her daughter to Sammy, for he, like all children, could interpret signals. Gulping on a mouthful of cake, he looked across the table at her, saying, 'I know why she wants you to walk about, Mrs B, it's so she can get her bet. Willie told me.'

As Fiona turned to look at her son she remembered: although she had told him that in no way was she having Sammy betting on her condition, she hadn't said that he mustn't tell Sammy about the silly business. And she had forgotten that those two were almost soul-mates.

'It's a silly business,' she said. 'It'll come when it's ready, not before and not after.'

'And it'll surprise everybody.'

They all looked at Sammy now, and it was Mark who said, 'What do you mean, it'll surprise everybody?'

'Well –' Still looking at Fiona, Sammy answered, 'Babies are surprises, aren't they? And people brag about 'em bein' big. So yours will be a surprise.'

Fiona smiled down at Sammy. He came out with such odd things, did this small rough child. But she was to remember his words. Oh, yes, very vividly she was to remember his words.

Sammy was now looking at Willie and saying, 'Mrs Fuller, upstairs, was gona have a bairn. It was the time me ma was with us an' she said she was pig-sick of listening about it. But Mrs Fuller had three all at one go! Me ma said she should have hired a sty 'cos she'd had a litter.'

'Stop it! All of you, stop it! You'll have your teas over.'

'Sammy!' Fiona had to swallow deeply in order to keep a straight face and insert admonition into his name. And the boy, recognising this, said, 'I never swored, Mrs B.'

Both Katie and Mark took this up: looking at their mother and spluttering, they said, 'I never swored, Mrs B,' which caused Sammy to round on them. His face red, he started, 'Aw, you lot are silly bug. . . .' But like a crack of the whip his name came back at him: 'Sammy!'

'Aw well!' He tossed his head. 'They're takin' the mickey.'

'Only because you're funny, Sammy.'

Mark stretched out his arm behind Willie's back to pat Sammy on the shoulder, saying, 'If we didn't like you we wouldn't rib you.'

'He's right. He's right.' Willie was nodding at his friend now. 'It's because we like you that we can rib you.'

'Well, I wish you didn't like me so much, then I'd know where I stood.'

It was Fiona's turn to smile, but quietly, down on the boy. He might only be nine, the same age as Willie, but he was keen-witted, likely due to his rough upbringing. And the thought made her wonder what he would turn out to be because she couldn't see the polish of the private school sinking deep. And perhaps, after all, that was a good thing.

Of a sudden Katie said, 'There's a car come on the drive. It'll be Dad.'

'A car? I never heard a car. It must be the wind.'

'If cuddy's lugs says it's a car, it's a car,' Mark said as he got up from the table.

Before he reached the hall the bell rang and, looking over his shoulder at his mother, he said, 'She was right.'

When he opened the door Fiona was behind him, and on seeing Rupert Meredith standing there she paused before greeting him: 'Oh . . . hello! Do come in. It's a wild night. Take Mr Meredith's coat, Mark.'

'I hope I'm not intruding. Is it meal time?' He looked at Mark, and the boy answered, 'Oh, we're finished, sir. Would you like a cup of tea?'

'Well. . . .'He looked at Fiona, and she said, 'Yes, he would. Would you see to it, Mark?'

'Yes. Yes, Mam.'

'Come into the dining-room; there's a proper fire in there. Bill hates artificial logs. He's going to have the sitting-room fireplace out, he says. But I like my artificial logs; I can switch them on any time I'm feeling cold.'

Rupert stopped just within the doorway of the dining room and, looking towards the table, he said, 'Oh, I am intruding; you're all set for dinner.'

'It's only for Bill and me. You see, he's rarely in nowadays before half-past six, and of late it's been sometimes nearly eight. So we've had to go back to our old system of feeding the tribe at tea-time. We tried for a while to have our meal as a family but they got so hungry they kept stuffing themselves while they waited.'

'I like this room,' he said, looking about him. 'It always appears to me very cosy. The dining-room at Brookley Manor is a fine room, but it's much too big for the three of us. It's different when the family come.'

'Do sit down.' She pointed to a winged upholstered armchair to the side of the fire; but he declined, saying, 'No, no; you take that seat. It looks so comfortable.'

'I prefer a straight-backed one.' She smiled at him and

44

turned one of the dining-room chairs round towards the fire. 'It's easier for me to get up . . . and down.'

'How are you feeling?'

'Well, very well, extremely so.'

'That's good. I told Lady Kingdom I might look in after I left Newcastle, and she wishes me to convey her best wishes to you and hopes that you are not feeling too uncomfortable. Those were her words. Apparently from what she says, she had a very bad time with all her children. And as Sir Charles pointed out, he's had a very bad time with them all since then. You know Sir Charles!'

'Yes.' She nodded. 'How is he?'

'Oh, he seems to have got a new lease of life. I think it's the interest engendered by the site. He trots down every possible opportunity. I think the men must sometimes imagine he's snooping to see if they are working or not; but he seems to have caught your husband's enthusiasm and excitement. He really is much better than he's been for years, I should say. In fact, this time last year he wouldn't have thought of travelling to Scotland, but that's where they're off to at the end of the week. His younger brother is in rather a low state and apparently they're worried about him at yon end. So he feels he must go. And he might stay over Christmas, that is if he can get round Lady Kingdom. He just does not enjoy the Christmas gatherings at home. As you know, he has a horde of grandchildren and, like all children, when space offers they run wild. For my part I look forward to their coming.'

'Why have you never thought of marrying?'

Almost as she was saying this she was chiding herself for probing. Yet the question had been on her mind for some time: here was this man, on thirty years old, handsome, because that was the word for him, and charming, and he had the kindest manner, the kindness was expressed in his eyes, deep brown like the colour of his hair. He wasn't all that tall, about the same height as Bill, five-foot-ten. And

45

so, when she received no answer to her question and saw that his gaze was now levelled towards his crossed knees, she said, 'I'm sorry. If that wasn't impertinent it must at least have appeared nosy. I'm sorry.'

'*Oh, no, no.* Please don't be sorry; and you would never be impertinent. But to answer your question: I have thought of marriage, very, very often, but there's . . . well, an impediment. I'll tell you about it some time. Now I'm going to be sort of impertinent when I say, may I call you Fiona? It's a lovely name, Fiona. And my name is Rupert, as you know.'

Oh, dear, dear, dear. There was a little hammer hitting her on the head, saying, 'Bill. Bill. Bill. You must understand it means nothing; we've known him for months; it's natural that we should be on more familiar terms.'

'I'm sorry. I should not have asked.'

'Oh yes. Don't be silly. Well, what I mean is, we've known each other for some time now and quite candidly, I don't like the sound of Mrs B. . . .Ah!' She paused and looked towards the door. 'Mark with your tea; and all set out on a tray I hope you'll notice.'

'I do indeed. And some cake too. Thank you very much, Mark.'

'I wouldn't be too thankful for the cake, sir; it's a bit dry.'

As Rupert laughed Fiona said, 'I suppose you have noticed by now that I have a very frank and outspoken family.'

'Yes, and I find it very refreshing.'

'By the way, Mam.' Mark was looking at his mother now. 'Sammy is about to take his leave and he wants to say goodbye, or so long, or ta-ra. You may take your choice. He has to get home and set the tea for his father.' This last was addressed to Rupert, and he, looking at Fiona, said, 'Does he come every day?'

'Most days. But he'll always be welcome.'

'Yes, yes, of course.'

'Let him come in before he goes,' she said to Mark.

'Will do.'

When they had the room to themselves again, she looked at her visitor and asked, 'Does Sir Charles ever hear of Mrs Brown?'

'Yes; he hears of her but not from her; nor does he want to. But I do know he wrote her a very severe letter – I typed it – and it was to the effect that she should be serving a sentence of eight years alongside her two stooges. And it went on to say, he never wanted to set eyes on her again and that if she attempted to come back into this country he would put the police on her. It took a great deal for him to dictate that letter. But I put it down word for word as he said it. It was sent to her London agent, for he would likely know where to send it. But it was strange, when I was up in town a few months ago, I called on him with the intention of trying to find out if she had really tried to come back into this country, because there was really nothing to stop her, no warrant was out for her arrest and those two villains had kept quiet as to who was paying them to ruin your husband's business. But the fellow had moved. Still, Sir Charles will be ever grateful to your husband for not pressing the case against her, because if she had to go to prison I'm sure it would have had a dire effect on him; he had been dotingly fond of her; as Lady Kingdom had said more than once, he thought more of her than he did of his own daughters, and all because he considered she'd had a dirty deal in having to marry Brown.'

Fiona did not remark on this, thinking, and naturally as she knew Bill would have done, that of the two Browns he was more to be pitied. Although he was an objectionable creature and had had it in for Bill, she doubted if he would have dared go to the lengths that she had, simply because her overtures had been spurned, yes, and that was the right word in both cases, overtures and spurned, by a man like Bill.

47

When there was the sound of a commotion in the hall she thought with something akin to panic, Oh dear, no! not Bill, and *him* here.

But it was Bill. The door opened slowly and he walked in slowly, and on his appearance Rupert stood up, saying, 'Here I am again, scrounging tea.'

'Aye, I see that.' Bill now walked towards Fiona, but, as would have been usual, he didn't bend and kiss her; instead, sitting on a chair near her, he said, 'Windy outside.'

'Yes; it's been blowing a gale all day. I'll go and get you a cup of tea.'

He put out his hand and stayed her movement, saying, 'It's all been put in order; they're seein' to it. Well –' he looked at Rupert, who was now seated again, and asked, 'And what are you doin' with your life these days?'

'Oh, much the same as usual: ferrying my boss, doing his mail, running errands, the same routine.'

'Good life if you can get it.'

Rupert reached out now, picked up his cup and drained it; then putting it back on the tray, he said, and in a voice from which all pleasantness had disappeared, 'It isn't the work I would have chosen, but circumstances in some cases take no account of desires. Well –' his tone changed slightly as he got to his feet and, looking at Fiona, said, 'I must be off; but I'll be able to tell Lady Kingdom that you're still feeling well. Good-night, Fiona.'

She did not rise as she said, 'Good-night . . . Rupert.'

'I'll see you out,' said Bill.

'There's no need; I can find my way. You must be tired after your day's work. Good-night.'

When the door closed on him, there was silence between them, until Fiona burst out, 'How could you, Bill!'

'How could I what? Come in here and find you tête-à-tête, that's the term isn't it, tête-à-tête? all cosy an' nice, and now on top of that it's Fiona and Rupert. It was Mrs B last time, if I remember, and Mr Meredith.'

'Well, now it's Fiona and Rupert as you say; so what do you make of it?'

'What I've made of it afore, just that he doesn't come here to convey messages from Lady Kingdom to you, or from you to her; he comes to see you and you're pleased to see him.'

'Yes, Bill, yes, let's face facts, I'm pleased to see him.'

'*Fiona!*' He was standing in front of her. 'I told you afore we married, didn't I, what would happen if anybody came between us, ever, didn't I? And I wasn't shoutin' me head off when I told you. When I'm really serious about anything I never shout, and I'm not shoutin' now.'

As she stared up into his face she knew a moment of fear. No, he wasn't shouting and she knew he meant what he said. Her voice was trembling now as she answered, 'That being the case, you must tell him not to visit here any more.'

'No, not me, but you. You must tell him.'

Her throat was tight; the muscles in her stomach seemed to be throwing the child from side to side. She cleared the restriction in her throat before she said, 'I never thought I would say this to you, Bill, but at this moment I don't like you. I still love you but I don't like you.' And at this she pulled herself up from the chair and, almost thrusting him aside, she went from the room. And he didn't stop her.

It was only a matter of minutes later when Katie came into the room and stood by the chair in which he was sitting, his elbows on his knees, staring into the fire.

'Mam's crying. . . .Did you hear what I said, Dad? Mam's crying.'

He pulled himself upright. 'Yes, I heard what you said, Katie.'

'Why have you made her cry?'

'It was something you wouldn't understand.'

'Oh yes, I would, and I do.'

He turned his head sharply and looked at her, and she

went on, 'It's because you found Mr Meredith here, isn't it? You're jealous because he's different from you.'

'*Katie*. Now mind. You can go so far.'

'But it's the truth, isn't it? I'm not a little girl, Dad. Well, I mean I am, but you know I was here when you first came and we all loved you and we still love you . . . more. And Mam loves you. But even if her stomach is sticking out a mile, she's still attractive, and you don't like that, do you?'

He now dropped his head onto his chest and moved it slowly.

'Don't be mad at me.'

He was looking at her again as he said, 'I'm not mad at you, lass, I'm only amazed that you seem so grown up and so different from the little girl I knew when I first came into this house. Well, this being so, and being observant as you are, you know me, so you'll know that I can't change. I am what I am, brash, loud-mouthed, ambitious, but protective of me own. Aye, those are the words. I read them some-where, but they apply to me. I'm protective of me own. And Katie' – he put his hand out now and laid it gently on her shoulder – 'I know something that you don't know, as yet. I know men and the workings of their minds. Sometimes I'm wrong, but not very often. Ninety-five to five, I'd say.'

Katie's eyelids were blinking rapidly, and in this moment she looked very much like her mother as she said, 'Go on up and tell her you're sorry.'

'No, pet. I'll go up, aye, and tell her I love her, but not that I'm sorry for what I said, for if he comes here again I'll give him the same cool reception, colder, being *me*, you know.' He smiled grimly now.

Reaching up, Katie placed her lips on his stubbly cheek, saying, 'You're a funny man, Bill Bailey, but I love you.'

He put his arms about her and held her close for a moment, then said, 'Go and see to the dinner. I'll bring her down.'

'Perhaps she'll like it on a tray. She may have gone to bed.'

'Aye, she might. A tray would be fine.'

She had hardly left the room when Mark came in and, purposefully but in a low voice, said, 'Dad, Mum's gone into her room. She's crying.'

Bill's voice was louder now. 'Yes, Mark,' he said, 'I know your mother's gone into her room cryin'. And I'm cryin' an' all inside. So what does a man do when he's cryin' inside, can you tell me? Now your sister Katie who's grown up. . . .*Oh, yes, she is*. Don't shake your head like that. She's very much grown up. Her remedy for cryin' is to say you're sorry. What's your remedy?'

It seemed a long moment before Mark said, 'Well, you sort of have to arrange things and your life and that so you never have to say you're sorry.'

'Oh my God! boy.' Bill gave him one hard slap on the back. 'You're goin' to break under the lessons you've got to learn, whereas Katie, she'll ride the waves. But don't worry, for as the sayin' goes, it'll all come out in the wash. Now go and help Katie put out the dinner for us. Tell her I want two trays upstairs, and you give her a hand.'

Mark stood where he was and watched Bill stalk from the room, and what he thought was, He's a funny man, really. I don't think he understands Mam.

3

Saturday afternoon was grey and icy cold. The sky was low and heavy and the forecast, everyone said, was snow; and yet it was only the end of November.

Bill was driving back home from the outskirts of Durham; he was feeling very pleased with himself: he had, as he thought, killed two birds with one stone. The first was reposing in the glove box. It was Fiona's Christmas box and in it lay, on a velvet pad, a heavy filigree gold necklace with matching ear-rings. They had been handwrought by a young artist and, as he put it to himself, had cost him a bomb. But what did it matter as long as they pleased her. The notion had entered his mind when watching her face as she was looking at the picture of some actress attending a gala: Katie, who was sitting beside her, had said, 'Look at that necklace she's wearing, Mam. Isn't it beautiful?' and Fiona had murmured, 'Yes, indeed; and I bet it was a beautiful price too.' Well, it had been a beautiful price. That young gold-smith was maybe just starting out but he knew his own worth. Still, what odds; he was making money now and he'd make more.

Then there was the house. Twice in the last week he had been over to see it. The first time he had just walked round the garden, all five acres of it. But on Wednesday he had made an appointment with the agent to view the house itself; the people were still in it. And by! as soon as he had stepped into that hall he knew that this was where he would want to bring Fiona and the family. It wasn't a baronial hall in any sense, quite modern in fact; well, the whole house had been modernised thirty years ago and the man had done a good job on it: the mouldings on the ceilings had been retained, as also had the eighteen-inch skirting boards; and all doors were solid hard wood. But the furnishings, especially the carpets and drapes, were modern and beautiful. The whole house was beautiful. Three of the six bedrooms were en suite. And there was an indoor swimming-pool with dressing-rooms. My! My! He could see them all there, the whole family, with Sammy Love, too. Aye, Sammy Love, too. It wasn't strange, he was continually telling himself, that that boy's name should pop into his mind: if ever there was a saviour it was Sammy Love.

Roll on Monday. He smiled to himself. Katie was going to lose her bet. He could picture her handing over the five pounds and him taking it and pocketing it, at least for a time. That would teach her a lesson. He loved Katie. He loved them all. But love alone didn't express his feelings for Fiona, adoration was nearer the mark. And he had sworn to himself never to upset her again as he had done the other night. By! she was in a state. And so was he. Oh, aye, he was an' all. Funny about cryin': it was more painful when you cried inside; you got relief when you could let the water flow.

Blast it! He had taken the country road off the roundabout. It was that bloody lorry driver. *Maniacs!* Likely the same bloody hit-and-run one that had finished Mamie's Mam and Dad and her brother.

Being a country road, he could have turned back, but he kept on although it would put another couple of miles on the journey. Had it been a pleasant day he would have enjoyed this run. The road must have gradually been rising, for it opened onto a stretch of moor. Here it was bordered on one side by a ditch and on the other by a wire fence.

He had travelled about a mile and a half along this stretch before seeing another vehicle, but there, in the far distance was one seeming to be travelling in the same direction. Presently, however, he realised that the car was stationary and was parked half on the road and half towards the fence.

He slowed down, wondering if there were anything wrong, and in such an out-of-the-way place.

There was something very familiar about the car, an elderly Rolls, at least as much of it as he could see, for one side of the bonnet was up and the driver was bending over the engine.

He stopped and, putting his head out of the window, shouted, 'Got trouble?'

When the figure straightened up and turned towards him and said, 'Yes, you could say that,' they both stared at each other for a moment. Then Bill, getting out of the car, walked forward, saying, 'You're out of your way this end, aren't you?'

'No, no; I often take this road.'

'But Brookley Manor is over there in that direction.' He pointed.

'Yes, I know where Brookley Manor is, but I wasn't going to Brookley.' Rupert Meredith's tone was stiff, and when he looked at his wrist-watch Bill said, 'Been here long?'

'Oh, about five minutes.'

It was obvious that the fella, as Bill termed him, seemed to be on tenterhooks, looking first up the road, then down. 'You expectin' help?' he asked.

'No. Where would I get help on this road except from passing motorists.'

'Aye.' Bill gave a small laugh. 'There's that in it. Well, can I be of any help to you? Where do you want to go?'

54

The younger man now stared at Bill for some moments before he said simply, 'Hetherington.'

'Hetherington? You . . . you mean the hospital?'

'Yes, I mean the hospital, or as some would still call it, the lunatic asylum.'

'Aye, well.' For a moment Bill seemed taken aback; then he said, 'Well now, I should ask why, but I'm not goin' to. Anyway, I would lock her up.' He pointed to the car. 'And on our way there we should find a garage and ask them to pick her up. But I'd like to bet Sir Charles won't welcome the news that his baby has broken down.'

'It won't be the first time; she's getting worse for wear.'

'How is he, by the way?'

'He was very well when I put him and Lady Kingdom on the train for Scotland this morning.'

'Oh, they've gone to Scotland then?' They were both sitting in Bill's car now and as he started her up he added, 'What's takin' them up there at this time of the year? I thought he didn't like the cold.'

Rupert didn't enlighten him on this subject, and they drove in silence for some way until they came to a country crossroads, when he said, 'If you turn sharp right here it will bring you to the gates. And there's a garage just beyond.'

'I've never been on this road before. I thought I knew this part very well. You live and learn.'

'That is quite true. And when one is living and learning I should like to tell you now that I have no designs on your wife.'

The car jerked as if it were going over a grid as his mind said, 'That's straight from the shoulder anyway.' But the actual words that came out, and in a casual tone, were, 'Well, you surprise me. Still, accept that's so, why then your frequent visits?'

'Because I found it pleasant to talk to someone of my own age, and a woman. Sir Charles and Lady Kingdom are the dearest people in the world but they are of another generation and one again removed. And there isn't what you would call a home life in the Manor, except when the family bring their children; whereas in your home there is a liveliness, and with the added attraction of amusing youngsters like Master Sammy Love.'

'If you feel like that then, why haven't you a wife of your own? Why aren't you married?'

'Fiona asked me the same question.'

The very fact that the fella was calling his wife by her Christian name and in that voice of his stirred something in his bowels, but he forced himself to say, 'What answer did you give her?'

'I told her I would tell her sometime.'

'Are you normal, I mean . . .?'

Even Bill himself had to admit he couldn't have bawled any louder than the fella when he cried, 'Yes! I am normal. And yes! I know what you mean.'

'You can shout almost as well as me.'

'You're an insulting bug-ger, aren't you?'

Bill suddenly wanted to laugh. It was the way he said, bug-ger; it sounded so fancy, it wasn't like bugger at all. 'I don't know about being an insultin' bugger; I'm a plain one, I say what I think.'

'Well, I think it might pay you in future to think before you speak.'

'Now look here!'

'No, you look here, *Mr Bailey*. I have no need to explain anything to you, but here we are at the hospital and I thank you for the ride. You need not wait for me. There is a garage quite near, I can walk there.'

'Just as you like.'

He drew up the car outside the high iron gates, and when Rupert got out, Bill watched him walk towards the small wicket gate and speak to a uniformed man standing there, then go towards the window of an office, where he stood for

56

a few moments before striding away up the drive towards the hospital that was out of sight beyond the trees.

He turned the car around, but then drew it along by the side of the high wall and in such a position that he could keep his eye on the gate. Why should this fella be going to Hetherington? Some people called the place a nerve hospital, while others gave it its old name of asylum. But then, why should he be goin' there? Well, in the ordinary way you would have thought he would have gone to Scotland with Sir Charles and Lady Kingdom, 'cos it seemed at times that the old fella couldn't get on without him. Had he a parent in there, a mother or a father, or some relative that he felt responsible for?

He recalled that in the car he would keep looking at his wrist-watch, and he seemed agitated, so much so that his suave gentlemanly manner had slipped and he had reacted to the pointed questions just as he himself might have done.

He, too, looked at his watch. It was twenty minutes to three. How long would he likely be in there? Well, he would give him an hour. Aye, he would; he would give him an hour. Fiona wouldn't be worrying because he had told her he was going out shopping for Christmas boxes for the bairns before all the shops were sold out.

He switched on the radio; but after a minute or so switched it off.

That fella wasn't so soft and pliable as he looked. But then, soft wasn't the right word, perhaps courteous would be better. Still, courteous or pliable, he could swear. And he smiled to himself as he said aloud, 'Bugger.' Then for him to come out with, 'I have no designs on your wife.' No beating about the bush there.

But who had he gone in there to see? Someone connected with him or perhaps with the old boy? Aye. Yes, that was a possibility. That's why he had stayed behind, to carry out the visits.

Oh hell! If he had an hour to spare, surely he could find

57

something better to do than sitting here. By! he could that. It was weeks now since he had given himself a day off; even on Sundays he kept at it.

It would be today, when he hadn't a newspaper or book in the car. Had the kids left anything in the back? He leant over the back of the seat and groped in the paper rack and pulled out a square hard-backed book and smiled as he looked down on it. It was one of Mamie's, entitled, *Nancy Nutall And The Mongrel*. Where on earth did these writers get their titles? The pictures were nice. Mamie loved this book.

He started to read the little story. It didn't take long, and he found himself amused that the last words of most of the little chapters were: 'And Nancy's father sighed again.'

Apparently Mr Nutall was sighing over his daughter because she was in her way demanding a dog and his wife didn't like dogs. . . .He'd have a daughter soon, or a son. Somehow he fancied a daughter. Of course, a son could follow in his footsteps. He could see himself taking him to football matches; that's if the crowd weren't wearin' steel helmets by then. Well, a cricket match then. And that was getting as bad. He could see himself reflected in the windscreen nodding at himself, and he smiled. This is what happened when you were left on you own, sitting in a car waiting, because the fella could have got a taxi quite easily at the garage.

But what if he did have a daughter? Well, as he said, he would call her Angela; and he would watch her growing up into another Katie, but with a difference: she'd be his, his own daughter. Looking back down his family line, he had to admit that they weren't good breeders. His father had been an only child, his mother one of twins and the twin had died. And what he remembered of his grandmother, she'd been a loner too. Anyway, he'd be quite satisfied with one, whatever sex. But being satisfied with one wasn't going to stop him trying again. Oh no. And Fiona, bless her, was more than willing. By! he'd got a prize there; and he meant to hang onto it. And the thought brought him back to the man who had gone up to the hospital.

How long had he been sitting here now? Over half an hour. Well, as he'd said to himself, he would give him an hour.

He switched on the radio again: a sports commentator was yelling his head off over a motor-cycle race. He lay back in the seat, pulled his tweed cap over his brow and prepared to doze, only immediately to pull himself upright again and look out the rear window. That was a daft thing to do, he told himself; the temper that fella was in he could have walked past him and left him sitting high and dry till the cocks crowed.

His watch said he had been sitting fifty minutes when he saw Rupert come out of the gate. And he noted that he neither looked to the right nor to the left but walked with his head down away from him as though making for the garage.

He tooted sharply on the horn, but had to repeat the process three times and start up the car before he saw the fella pause and look towards him.

He now turned the car about and stopped again alongside Rupert, and, leaning over and pushing open the passenger door, he called, and none too gently, 'Get in.'

Rupert did not immediately get into the car, but bending slightly, he said, 'You needn't have done this; I could easily get a taxi.'

'Get in. I'm bloody well froze. I suppose you know when these are stationary they don't give off heat.'

Rupert got into the car. But Bill didn't start up straight-away; he turned and looked at Rupert as he said, 'Well, put your seat-belt on. If we go out lookin' for an accident you'll go straight through the windscreen.'

They had gone about half a mile along the road, and Bill, glancing at his passenger, asked, 'You all right?'

'Yes. Yes, I'm all right.'

The words were said in the usual polite cultured tone; and Bill, ever forthright, said, 'Well, you don't look it. Where you makin' for?'

'Brookley. But . . . but drop me in the town; I can get a bus out.'

'Who's lookin' after you there?'

'I'm looking after myself. I'm used to it. Anyway, Jessie comes in every day.'

'Look; I'm sorry I opened me big mouth.' Even as he said it he was wondering why he should be apologising to this fella because he had to admit he was still furiously jealous of him; what he was and what he stood for he imagined must appeal to Fiona as they were pretty much of the same class.

'Do you mind stopping the car for a moment?'

'What do' you want me to stop the car for? Now look; just sit tight.'

'Please. I'm going to vomit.'

'Good God!' Bill didn't know whether he spoke the words or just thought them, but he pulled the car up to a jerking halt. And the next minute he watched the fella hanging onto a railing and vomiting onto the grass verge.

He went round the car to him, and as he was wont to do with the lads or Katie or Mamie under such circumstances, he put out his hands and held Rupert's head. And his face twisted into a grimace as the fella heaved as if he would bring his heart up.

When the bout was over he remained by Rupert's side as he leant against the railings and drew in long slow deep breaths. But when he seemed to be making no move Bill shivered and said, 'Come on; get yourself back into the car; it'll freeze you out here.' He did not, however, now attempt to assist him, but hurried round the car and took up his seat again, and remained seated quiet for a while; then said, 'You often car sick?'

60

There was a moment's hesitation before Rupert said, 'No; I'm never car sick.'

Again there was silence. And Bill noted that the fella lay back against the head rest and continued to take in the long deep breaths, after which he said, 'Take your time; there's no hurry.'

The silence hung heavy on him. There was no movement on the road, except for a passing car, and he sat looking straight ahead and down the long length of the road, waiting for the fella to say he was all right. But when he did speak it was to say, 'You asked why I never married. Well, the reason is back there. We were going to be married on her twenty-fourth birthday. We had been engaged for two years. We had actually known each other since our schooldays when she had come to stay with the Kingdoms because her people were abroad. There was a distant connection there. Then her parents split up. Her mother remarried and her father was killed in an accident. Her mother was then in America and wanted her to go, but she wouldn't leave me. We seemed to know from the start there was only each other. I had been through university and was interested in industrial design. Sue's stepfather was in big business in the US, and he had an opening for me once we were married. It was all set. Then one night we were at a party.' He paused and wiped his lips with his handkerchief. 'We were leaving early. I went round to get the car. They were chock-a-block and so it was a while before I could bring the car to the front of the house. She wasn't there. The police found her the next morning, in the shrubbery not far away. She had been raped, and hit on the head. Just one blow, apparently just one blow to stop her screaming. She was in a coma for days; and when she came out she screamed, and when she wasn't screaming she just sat perfectly still, so perfectly still, looking ahead. And she's never spoken since, until today. They generally phone me when the fits are bad because she calms down somewhat when I'm near her. They are chary about

61

giving her too many drugs in case she goes into that long sleep. But, today she called my name.'

He stopped talking, and for once in his life Bill could find nothing to say, until the silence screamed at him, and then he said, 'Well, that's a good sign if she called your name.'

'I thought so too, but the doctor didn't seem very impressed. He said he didn't want me to get my hopes up; it sometimes happened, but it signified little.'

'Tactful blokes, doctors. By the way, did they ever find the fella that did it?'

'Oh yes; and he's only got three years to go now.'

The way those last words were spoken sent a small shiver through Bill; but he understood the fella's feelings all right; he had felt the same towards those bastards who had tried to do him in, and even more towards the one that had paid them.

Rupert turned and said to him, 'Now you know why I'm not married and why I continue to carry on in this cissy job, as so-called secretary to Sir Charles.'

Again Bill could find nothing to say. He sat back in the seat and looked through the windscreen as he thought: This should be an object lesson to you, lad. Your mother was always saying you never knew what was going on behind the curtains next door. People, himself included, envied those like Sir Charles and Lady Kingdom and this fella here for their position, their money, their houses, probably imagining that those things protected them from the tragedies of life. In fact, now he came to think about it the tragedies hit them harder than most because they put a face on it; people like himself yelled out against injustice, the injustice of tragedy, especially when it was doled out to the innocent like this fella's lass. God! that must have been awful.

Tentatively now, he asked, 'Were they long in finding the bloke?'

'No, no; the next day.'

'As *quick* as that?'

'Well, it was easy. You see, he was a friend, in fact, our very good friend. He had always fancied Sue. How he had got her to the shrubbery will never be known. It was suggested that he might have said, Come on let's hide from old Rupert. And she was high-spirited and mischievous. From what came out at the trial he hadn't meant to hit her, that was the last thing on his mind; but when she screamed he was afraid she'd be heard, and when she wouldn't stop screaming he put his hand across her mouth and his other hand, groping, must have come across the piece of wood. They showed it in court. It was only about a foot long but it had dark patches on it. He got ten years and he left the dock crying.

He let out a long-drawn sigh as if he was tired, but his voice was still level as he went on, 'He wouldn't have got that for rape alone. But the verdict of the specialist was that there was extensive brain damage, and although she had come out of the coma it was doubtful whether she would ever return to normal.'

He turned and looked at Bill now. 'Love's a funny thing. He had told his solicitor that he loved her and he couldn't bear the thought of me having her. And there we had been for three years, almost like brothers: playing squash together, cricket, tennis; him staying at the Manor, me staying with his family. Oh, yes, yes' – he nodded – 'he had a warm family. It finished them too: his father had a heart attack and died three days after the case was closed; his sister and her husband went off to Australia, and the mother's now at a cottage somewhere in Dorset, likely waiting for his return . . . as I am.'

Bill put a hand out and gripped Rupert's knee, saying, 'Forget that part, lad; but I know how you feel. Retribution is me second name and I know how I've longed to lay me hands on Sir Charles's pet god-daughter, but it's not worth it. Anyway, have you looked ahead? You can't go on like this: you're a young fella an' you need a family. You've already shown that to me. You must get yourself married.'

'I can't do that.' Rupert's voice was quite calm now. 'I somehow still think she'll come round sufficiently to recognise me, and what would happen then if I had a wife? I know I would leave her, no matter who she was, and go to Sue. You see, our relationship was something rare. We often discussed it. We felt we had been here before because we recognised each other right away when we were very young. And so I have memories, wonderful memories.'

'You can't live on memories, lad. Sometime or other they go sour on you. Anyway, let me say now, thanks for tellin' me. And I'm sorry about the big mouth of mine. But you see I'm as jealous as hell of Fiona; but not any more, where you're concerned.' He patted Rupert's knee. 'So, let's get home.'

'No, no. Please drop me.'

'Shut up! The matter's closed, except to say this: you're welcome there any time of the day or night; so fasten that seat-belt and let's get away. I know a good firm I can ring to pick up the Rolls.'

Rupert did not demur: he fastened his seat-belt, laid his head back on the rest once again, and did not speak for the rest of the journey.

On entering the house, Bill was saying to him, 'Get your coat off,' when there was a howl from upstairs that brought their attention to the landing; at the same time the kitchen door opened and Fiona came into the hall, and the commotion on the landing gave her a shield to cover the surprise of seeing whom Bill had brought with him after the fiasco of the other day.

'I'll bash your face in!'

'*Willie!*' Fiona and Bill cried almost simultaneously while looking up the stairs.

'Well, she's torn up my picture, Mam.'

'It was a picture of me' – Katie was now slowly descending

the stairs, her chin thrust out, battle blazing in her eyes – 'and he gave me a big nose.'

'No, I didn't! No bigger than it is. And a big mouth an' all.'

'Come down here, both of you.' Bill's voice was not loud now.

'Shan't.' This was from Willie, and he was about to turn away when a sound emanating from Bill's mouth shook them all and brought his stepson to a halt, his hand now gripping the top of the bannister.

'*Down!*' Bill thumped the floor three times, crying, 'Get down here this minute!'

Katie, now at the foot of the stairs, said, 'He's always taking the mickey out of me with his drawings and . . . .'

'And you, madam, get into the kitchen and find something to do with your hands instead of using your tongue so much. *Get!*'

After a very surprised look at her hero, Katie departed for the kitchen, but not in a hurry.

Then there was Willie, chin thrust out too; and to him Bill said, 'Get into that study. And the next time you say shan't to me, you won't be able to walk there.'

Willie hesitated, about to appeal to his mother, but by her look he thought better of it and stamped away. And Bill himself was about to turn to Fiona when another voice piped from the landing, 'They've been fighting all afternoon.'

'And you, madam, stop tellin' tales and get back to the playroom if you don't want your backside smacked.'

'Bill!' Fiona's voice was scarcely above a whisper and he turned to her and said, 'And you, madam, shut up!'

Before Fiona could either walk away or retort there was a sound from Rupert that made them both look up the stairs again and to the figure descending.

'Well, well, well.' Bill looked at Sammy and Sammy looked at him as, unblinking, he marched down the stairs.

'I didn't know you were here. Where've you been hidin'?'

65

'I ain't been hidin'.' Sammy passed Bill and made his way towards a chair to the right of the door on which his coat and cap were lying.

'Where do you think you're goin'?'

'I'm goin' home.'

'Where's your dad?'

'He's at the football match. Where else?'

Bill bit on his lip. 'Will he be home for tea?'

'How do I know? 'tis Saturda', isn't it?'

'Well, to tell the truth, Sammy Love, I don't know which day it is, it could be whistle-cock-Monday, nor do I know which end of me's up in this house. So don't you add to my confusion, but put that coat down again and get yourself into the kitchen and see if you can be useful and rattle up some tea. . . .Go on, get!'

Sammy stared at him for a moment, then slowly threw his coat and cap onto the chair, mumbling something as he did so.

'What did you say?'

The small boy turned and looked at the three adults; then his eyes focussing on Fiona, he said, 'He does nowt but shout.'

'Bill!' She caught at his arm; then on a half laugh, she said, 'And he's right. I'm sorry, Rupert.' She had turned towards him, but before he could answer, Bill said, 'Oh, don't be sorry for him; he wants a noisy family. Look, get yourself in there and sit down, and take him along with you.'

In amazement, Fiona looked from the one to the other and was surprised to see a quiet smile on Rupert's face, especially when he said, 'You'd better do what you're told.'

But before making a move to do what she was told she said to Bill, 'And what are you going to do?'

'I'm going into the kitchen to sort that lot out and get us some tea. We're both froze; it's cold outside you know.'

Bill now stamped towards the kitchen, and Fiona walked

66

into the sitting-room followed by Rupert. But she had hardly entered the room before she turned to him and said, 'I'm all at sea. What's happening? He was civil to you.'

'Oh, it's a long story, one for a winter's afternoon. And it's already been told. I'll leave it to Bill to relate to you, perhaps when you're tucked up in bed tonight.'

She sat on the couch; and when he sat down beside her and took her hand she glanced over the back towards the door; and when he said, 'It's all right. It's all right; he won't mind,' she stretched her face, her eyes wide, and said, 'No? Well, life is full of surprises.'

'Yes, isn't it,' he said; 'and some are nice.'

Bill did tell her the story when they were in bed tucked up together. And when he finished she was near to tears and she said, 'Poor soul. Oh, poor soul.'

'Now don't get too sorry for him,' he said; 'he's not goin' to fall for you, and you'd better not start fallin' for him because you know what I once promised you if you ever turned your eyes away from my direction – and I meant it, I wasn't jokin' – I'd murder you both.'

'Oh Bill! you do say such frightful things. But I'm glad you won't mind him coming here, for I sensed he was lost in some way. We'll have him for Christmas, eh?'

'Aye. Well, yes, that's an idea. . . .What is it? Got a pain?' He took his arms from around her and pulled himself up on an elbow, and she flapped her hand at him, saying, 'No, not really; no, just he, she, it, is jumping about a bit. Been doing it all day.'

'Oh! woman.' He drew in a long breath. 'I wish it was over; me nerves are in a frazzle; in fact, you've got all our nerves in a frazzle. That's what's the matter with the kids: they're all waitin'; they're tired of waitin'; their tempers are all on edge. And it's true, you know. You know what Willie said to me tonight when I was goin' for him? He started to bubble and he said, "I'm frightened." And when I said,

"What are you frightened about?" he said, "'Cos Mam's going into hospital and she mightn't come out." "Don't be daft," I said; "she's just goin' to have a baby. They all come out after havin' babies." And he said, "Do they?" And when I said, "Aye, yes of course," he said, "I hope it isn't a girl. I couldn't stand another Katie and another Mamie. Girls are awful." Then he ended up by sayin', "Sorry I cheeked you, Dad."' He sniffed; then laughed. 'That got me. That got me. He's a nice kid is Willie. They're all nice kids. I love em', but I've got to say it' – he laid his hand gently on her stomach – 'this 'un'll be really mine. Can you understand that and how I feel about it?'

'Yes, dear, I can understand that perfectly,' she said.

4

Bill was in the office cabin going over a pile of invoices with his accountant, Arthur Milburn, when a rap came on the door.

'Right!' he called, without lifting his head; and when a man entered and approached the desk, Bill sat back in his chair and looked at his works manager in enquiry, saying, 'Yes, what is it now? I can tell by your face it isn't pleasant.'

Peter Honnington said, 'No, it isn't very pleasant. There's been a bit of a fracas on the Community Hall site with that big Irishman and one of the new fellas.'

'You mean Love?'

'Yes, that's who I mean.'

'What's he done?'

'He's knocked a fella about. Had to get an ambulance.'

'God! How did that happen? Why did you have to get an ambulance?'

'Because the fella needed an ambulance; he couldn't get up and he was bleedin' heavily from the nose.'

'How did it happen? I mean, what started it?'

'As far as I can gather the man Potter referred to Love's nationality in a derogatory way.'

Bill stared at Honnington. Honnington's attitude stuck in

69

his neck at times, particularly his pedantic way of speaking. He was good at his job, but when that was said, all was said.

'Was it really necessary to get an ambulance?' he asked. 'Simms does first aid and there's everything that's needed in the hut.'

'The man was almost unconscious, and I may as well tell you the police came on the heels of the ambulance.'

Bill rose from his chair. 'Have they taken Love?'

'No; they questioned him. It will all depend if Potter presses the charge. Anyway, I've wanted to speak about this fellow Love for some time. In my opinion he's not the right man to be in charge of others. There's too much –' he paused here before he added, 'merriment goes on.'

'What have you got against merriment? As long as it doesn't interefere with the work. . . . Has it in this case?'

Honnington pursed his lips. 'Not noticeably,' he admitted; 'but his gang don't seem to have any respect for him. What I mean is. . . .'

'Oh, my God!' Bill turned his head away. 'Which century do you think we're in, man? The whole lot of them have hardly got any respect for me that's noticeable. In my opinion a happy gang works better, and if they're happy they'll joke.'

'Well, that's your opinion, sir.'

'Aye, it is.'

'What are you goin' to do about him then . . . Love?'

'Nowt. Why should I? except have a word with him. If the police have come on the job, they'll have plenty to say to him.'

'In my opinion I don't think he's the man for the job.'

'Don't you? Well, we differ on that point an' all. Anyway, send him along an' we'll hear his side of it. And he'll have a side, I know that.'

'Oh, yes, yes; he'll have a side.' Honnington turned and went out, and Arthur Milburn, looking at Bill, said, 'I don't

70

like that fella, never have. And I think that's the opinion on the site. But there's one thing about him, and it's in his favour, he's straight. So far there's been no back-handers to the contractors that I know of, and so, of course, he's not liked in that quarter either.' He smiled. 'A man can't have it all ways, can he? Now back to the pounds, shillings, and pence.'

But Bill couldn't put his mind wholly to the pounds, shillings, and pence, because he was thinking that if that fella was sent along the line again to Durham it would do something to him. The bloody fool. It was to be hoped the other fella wasn't badly hurt.

It was not ten minutes later when a rap came on the door and Davey entered and, going straight to the desk, he got the first one in by saying, 'I know, boss, I know. I know every word that's gona come out of yer mouth, an' the first one is, you're a bloody fool, Love, you're a bloody fool. But I don't feel so in this case, boss. No, begod! I don't When I give you the rights of it you'll likely see me side.'

When he paused Bill said, 'All right; go ahead and give me the rights of it.'

Davey cast a glance at Arthur Milburn, then nodded at him, and looking back at Bill, he said, 'That bloke's been a trouble since you set him on, boss. The artful dodger he's known by. Boss, my crew had been a happy lot till Jack Potter was put among 'em. I'm tellin' you, boss, he's the kind of bloke what starts riots. Ireland is dotted with 'em: they're against everybody else's God but their own. And against Parliament, works managers, an' people who go abroad for their holidays. That's the kind of bloke he is. So you can guess, boss, what he thought of me. And he showed it. Oh aye, begod! he showed it. But I put up with it. Every day for the past week I've put up with it, since Jim Ridley went sick an' you put this one in his place. But to come to the point. Just an hour gone I asked him, and I did it, boss, as you told the lot of us who's in charge of gangs, ask first,

71

and if that doesn't work, then tell 'em. Well, I asked first. "Take those four-be-two's down to Roger," I said. Roger was workin' in a little room at the end, puttin' the floor in. If I'd asked the fella to climb up to the roof I could have understood it when he lifted one plank an' put in on his shoulder an' went to walk off. "What you playin' at?" I said next. "There's two more there on the floor beggin' to be lifted at one an' the same time." He stopped now and lifted another, then said, "It's me back."

'"Aye," said I; "we've all got backs, an' they ache. But you tell yours yer goin' to give it another plank an' see what it says." Well, boss, he lifted up the other plank and he muttered somethin'. And I guessed it wasn't in me favour, boss. So I said to him, "What was that you were after mutterin'?" And at that, you know what happened?'

Bill made a slight movement with his head, as did Arthur Milburn; and Davey, nodding from one to the other, said, 'He threw the three bloody planks at me. They scraped me shins. Look!'

He stepped back from the desk, pulled up his trouser leg, pushed down his sock, and there indeed Bill could see that the planks had scraped his legs and drawn blood for quite a long way down from below his knee.

Davey now said, 'I nearly fell on me arse; an' you can guess, boss, I let out an oath or two. Then there he was, standin' yellin' at me. And you know, boss, I'm quite used to people pointin' out me nationality – well me tongue gives me away – and I can laugh with 'em that chip me, but not this time, boss. You know what he said to me? He said, "You thick pig-ignorant Irish Paddy." That's what he called me. Then he went on to mention how the muck of the sty was runnin' out of me ears. God in heaven! I could stand no more. An' I heard no more, 'cos I went in at him hell for leather. I only had the chance to hit him three times for the lads got me off him. Then Mr Honnington came on the scene. An' there's a man who has no love for me either –

72

we don't speak the same language. No, begod! we don't, 'cos that man's so unbendin' you would think he has a poker up his. . . .'

'All right. All right.' As Bill raised his hand to check further description of where the poker might be, because he had heard it all before, he said, 'Have you thought what'll happen if that fella makes a case of it?'

'Aye, boss. Aye.' Davey turned sideways and looked towards the floor; then jerking his head up again, he said, 'But I couldn't do anythin' else, boss; 'twas more than flesh an' blood could stand. It didn't take very long, though, after I saw him lyin' there for me to know that they'll throw the book at me. Aye, begod! Second time for actual bodily harm, they'll throw the book at me all right. An' I'd like to bet they'll not take into account that the two blokes that are inside now doin' their time are only there 'cos I collared the first one, will they?'

'I don't know about that; but they might remember, Davey, that you knocked him about an' all.'

'Aye, well, he didn't miss me either, did he now? I was in a bit of a mess meself, wasn't I now?'

'But you're not this time, Davey, are you?'

'No,' Again Davey looked towards the floor. 'No,' he said, shaking his head; 'but, boss, nobody's goin' to get me to say I'm sorry for what I did. The only thing I'm sorry for –' and he now looked up at Bill again as he repeated, 'the only one thing I'm sorry for is the effect this is gona have on the lad: if I go along the line for however long or short a time, what'll happen to him?'

'I don't think you need worry about that part of it, at least what'll happen to him physically; it's what'll happen to him in his mind concernin' you. You should think about that, you big galoot.' Bill's voice had risen; and now leaning across the table and his hands splayed out flat on it, he stared up into Davey's distressed countenance as he repeated, 'You never stop to think.'

For a moment Davey didn't say anything; then he said, 'Can I ask you a straight question, boss?'

'Yes, go ahead.'

'If some bloke called you a big-mouthed Scouse, would you stand an' say, thank you very much?'

Bill sat back in his chair. He had something there. If anybody had used that term on him he knew that his reaction would have been just the same as the Irishman's 'What I would do is not in question,' he said. 'Perhaps I would have the sense to remember I had a wife and family to see to. You know, although you care for the lad you seem to forget your responsibility at times. Now, go on. I'll send somebody to the hospital to see how the fella's gettin' on. On your way, call in at E block and tell Bert Ormesby I'd like to see him for a minute.'

Davey didn't move, but he said, 'One last thing, boss. What'll happen if they come an' pick me up? I mean, about the lad. He won't go to his granny's on his own. He hasn't any feelin' for her nor her for him. But somebody'll have to take him an' tell her she'll have to put up with him.'

'You needn't worry on that score; he can pig in with Willie if it should be necessary. He'll be all right.'

'Aye, boss. Thanks. Aye, thanks.'

When the door closed on Davey, Arthur Milburn looked at Bill and, smiling, said, 'It's funny; even when that fella's in trouble you still want to laugh at him. He's got that way about him. I suppose it's like the comedian says, "It's how I tell 'em."'

But Bill was in no mood to concur. 'He's a bloody fool,' he said; 'and I've got enough on me mind at this moment without worryin' about him and his troubles.'

He now picked up the phone, and when the voice on the other end said, 'Fellburn 837260,' he said, 'You all right, dear?'

'Oh, yes. Yes, Bill.'

'Sure?'

74

'Sure.'

'No sign of it?'

'Not a murmur.'

He heard Fiona laugh before saying further, 'If it doesn't start today Katie's lost her five pounds.'

'Oh, aye. And mind, I'll take it. I'll tell her I'm not goin' to wait until she gets it out of the bank, so you loan it to her and we'll just watch her face when she hands it over, eh?'

'Oh yes; and she'll shed blood because she's been saving for as long as I remember.'

'Love.'

'Yes, Bill?'

'If . . . if there's any sign at all you'll give me a ring?'

'Please, please don't worry. Of course I will. You know I will. But the way I'm feeling I could go days.' Then her voice changing, she said, 'But I hope I don't; it's getting so heavy my legs are giving way. What would you say if they were all wrong and it's triplets?'

'Three hurrahs.'

'I had a card from Mother. It came just after you left. She had a wonderful journey; America is wonderful; the people are wonderful; she feels wonderful. I'm still very puzzled in that direction.'

'You're not the only one. I'll be home early.'

'You will?'

'Definitely. Just after five.'

'Good. Goodbye, dear.'

'Goodbye, love.'

'No sign of it yet?'

Bill shook his head in answer to Arthur Milburn, saying, 'She can't go on much longer; and she's tired. And so am I. I want this bairn badly, Arthur, but I don't think I could go through it again. I'm sure I couldn't.' And when Arthur Milburn burst out laughing, he said, 'You can laugh; it'll be your turn some day.'

'Not if I know it . . . not if I know it.'

75

'I said that once. Funny how circumstances make you change your mind. Aye.' He picked up his pen again. How circumstances make one change one's mind. He knew all about that.

The family were together in the sitting-room, Katie holding centre stage. She had just handed Bill five pounds and, as he sat looking at it on the palm of his hand, his face expressing surprise, Fiona put in quickly, 'Where did you get that, Katie?'

'From my bank.'

'But when?'

'When I was out on Saturday.'

'But . . . but I could have had the baby on Saturday, or yesterday, or even today.'

'I knew you wouldn't.'

'The oracle has spoken.'

'You shut up, our Mark.'

'Well! well!' Bill's voice brought Katie's attention from Mark. 'What made you so sure, hinny?'

'I don't know. I just felt . . . well, if the baby came, well and good, but if it didn't I wanted to have it ready, because I knew if I didn't . . . well, I mean have the money ready, Mam would offer to lend it to me supposedly and I would hand it to you; then at a convenient time you would hand it back. I didn't want that.'

'You didn't want me to hand it back?'

'No, I didn't; I'd . . . I'd made a bet and I wanted to stand by it. It was a matter of . . . well –' She jerked her head to the side, and when Mark put in, 'Ethics?' she glanced quickly at him and said, 'Yes, I suppose that's as good a word as any, but not what I meant.'

Fiona and Bill exchanged glances and Fiona thought, She's too young to think this way, too young to act like this; she'll be old before her time; while Bill thought, If the one that's coming is a girl and is a patch on her, she'll do.

Suddenly he put his arms out and jerked Katie into them, and when he kissed her she put her arms around his neck and leant against him for a moment, until Willie's voice brought her on the attack again as he said, 'Scene 101, retake, retake.'

'I will! I promise you I'll slap your face right and left.'

'Katie! And you, Willie.' Fiona drew in a long breath, then went on, 'I might as well tell you I'm getting very tired of your wrangling. At this moment I'm tired in all ways, but more so by the fact that you two are forever at each other's throats. What's the matter with you?' She was looking at Willie, and his answer was, 'Well, she must always be front of the picture. She's a know-all.'

'And you're a numskull and you'll never be at the front of the picture.'

'Right!' Bill's voice was not loud. 'I've heard enough and I'm ashamed of you both. Yes, I am at this minute, I'm ashamed of you both. There's your mam not knowin' where to put herself 'cos the waitin's gettin' her down, but what do you two do? Instead of being a comfort to her or tryin' to help you're goin' on like two guttersnipes. That's what you are, two guttersnipes.' He now pointed at Willie. 'Give Sammy Love the chance to be in your place and he wouldn't be actin' like you, I can tell you that. As for you, miss' – he was now pointing – 'there's two sides to you, and there's one of them I don't like. Now get yourselves away out of my sight and out of your mother's sight.'

'Bill – there was an appeal in Fiona's voice – 'let them be. They're on edge like me, like us all. Come here.' She held out her hands widely, and after a moment's hesitation they both walked towards her and she put her arms around them and looked from one to the other as she said, 'How can I go into hospital and feel at peace knowing that you two are likely to keep this up. Now I want you both to promise you'll call a truce, at least until I come back. Now! now! don't you dare say it's her.' And then turning towards

77

Katie, she said, 'And don't you dare say it's him. It's both of you; and you've got Mamie at it too because she takes her pattern from all you older ones.'

Then endeavouring to lighten the situation, Mark went up to Bill and said, 'I want to be loved an' all,' and pulled a face, but the answer he got was, 'You'll be loved, me boy, with a kick up the backside, and it'll be so hard that me boot'll knock your teeth out.'

At this, surprisingly Willie started to laugh and he turned his face into his mother's shoulder; Fiona, too, laughed, and Katie gave a wriggle.

'There's somebody in the hall.' Mark was hurrying towards the door when it opened and Nell entered.

'What's the matter? I thought you had gone home ages ago.'

'Of course I went home ages ago, but now I'm back; and so is Bert. He's in the kitchen with Sammy.'

With outstretched arm, Nell staved off Willie's dart for the door, saying, 'Stay! Stop! Remain where you are; all those three at once, Master William. This is your dad's business now. Anyway, what you all down here for?' She looked about. 'You should be upstairs. As for you' – she pointed to Fiona – 'why aren't you in bed?'

'I'm just about to go, Mrs Bossy Boots. But first of all I'm going into the kitchen.' She hung on to Bill's arm and he helped her up from the couch, Then, looking at the four children, she said softly, 'Stay where you are now. We'll come back and tell you what's happening.'

'You'll do nothing of the sort; you'll go straight upstairs following your kitchen visit, and I'll stay here and put this inquisitive lot in the picture.'

Bill had scarcely pushed open the kitchen door to let Fiona enter when Sammy's voice hit them both, saying, 'I'm not going to me granny's; I can stay by meself in our house. I'm used to stayin' by meself. If you send me to me granny's I'll only come back. 'Tis a waste of time.'

'Sit down. Sit down. Well what's the latest, Bert?'

'Well, boss, the fella must have pressed the charge. I told you I thought he was puttin' it on a bit. All right, his nose was broken and his lip's split but it would take more than a couple of punches to put a fella like him into shock. That's what the nurse said. I told you. I sort of put it to him when I saw him that Davey was sorry and that if he let the matter drop he wouldn't lose by it. But no. He's always appeared a spiteful individual since he first came on the job. Had a lot to say in the mess cabin, and by what I hear he's been in and out of more jobs than all the fellas put together. Anyway, Davey got word to me after tea. It was through one of the policemen. He brought Sammy along to ask if I would take him to his granny's. And the polis heard what Master Samuel' – he wagged his finger at the small boy – 'thinks about his granny. And when he emphasised the fact that he could stay alone, the polis wasn't having that. And so I said Nell and I would see to him. But he wasn't for staying with us either. So . . . well, boss, I thought I'd better come along and see if you had any ideas.'

'I'm not askin' to stay here, I'm not; I can stay by meself. I did it all the time.' The boy suddenly swung round and went towards the sink, yelling now, 'Bloody people! If they put me dad in prison I'll kick all the buggers to hell . . . I will! I will!'

'Here! Here! Enough of that!' Bill had swung him up now and through the air and planted him with a none too gentle plop on the chair. 'I thought you had left that language behind you. Goin' to a private school and comin' out with. . . .' He stopped at a signal from Fiona and, following her pointing finger, he noted now that tears were running down the face of the drooping head. And she addressed Bert in an overloud voice, saying, 'There'll be no need for Sammy to stay alone in his own house, Bert; he has stayed here with Willie before and he may stay again as long as he likes. Come on, Sammy.' She held out a hand towards him. But apparently he didn't see it. So she slowly stooped and picked up one of his from where it was hanging between his knees, and she led him, with his head bowed, from the room.

'We'll have to go and bail him out,' Bill said to Bert.

'Well, it's no use tonight, boss. I said those very words to the polis and he said nothing could be done until tomorrow morning when he'll be coming up before the magistrate. And he said a funny thing. He said that you'll be able to get him out if he pleads guilty, but if he pleads not guilty he'll go back inside and have to wait on his case coming up.'

'No!'

'Aye. That's apparently what the system is. Guilty and you're let out on bail, not guilty and you're kept in. Seems daft. But those are the very words the polis said.'

'Did he say what time or give you any idea when he'll come up?'

'Well, I understand they start at ten.'

Bill sighed. 'I'll be there then if it's possible. But what if something happens in the night?' – he thumbed towards the ceiling – 'in that case, you'll have to go and stand bail for him. Whatever the amount is put your name to it and I'll see to it. Anyway, Davey wouldn't scarper, at least I don't think so. But what I do know is, he's dead scared of Durham, and that being so, I don't understand why he doesn't control his bloody temper. Come on; let's go in and see how things are goin'. Talkin' of tempers, they've been flyin' here the night too. Master Willie's been on his high horse, so Mr Samuel Love's presence may do something to fetch him off it. Funny that. Talk about opposites clickin'; if ever there were two opposites they are it.'

What was he talking about, opposites clicking; if there were ever two opposites like Willie's mother and himself, they were it too. There was a lot to be said for opposites getting together.

Davey's case came up at eleven o'clock on the Tuesday morning. He pleaded guilty and was bailed on the assurance of five hundred pounds. The surety was one William Bailey.

A weak sun was shining when they came out of the court; and they walked along the street, neither of them speaking. And then Davey said, 'I never thought meself to be worth five hundred quid, boss. But I can assure you of one thing: you won't lose your money; I won't scarper. Even if I hadn't a youngster to see to I wouldn't scarper. But by God! I was sick to the bottom of me bowels in that cell last night. And I might as well tell you I've got a dread on me that's weighin' me down: just the thought of Durham turns me into a jelly, boss. It does. It does.'

'You're a bloody fool. You know that?'

'Aye, boss, I know that. But it's a way a man's built. I said afore, put yourself in my place on that day. I'm unlucky, that's me. I'm an unlucky sod. Here I am, fair set, a good steady job, a house that I never dreamt of, me kid at a private school. Eeh, my! that alone should make me think twice. But no, out goes me bloody fist. But why the eighth of January before the case comes up? Why couldn't they do it next week and I'd be out of me misery? I'd know one way or t'other.'

'Thank your stars you've got a little time to clear your head and get yourself a lawyer.'

'A lawyer?'

'That's what I said, a lawyer; for what d'you think you're going' to do? Talk to a judge and jury yourself?'

'Aye, I could, and do it better than some of those fellas.'

'So you think. But it's a lawyer you want, and we'll have to look around.'

'Is he still in hospital, the bloke?'

'No; as far as I can gather he came out this morning.'

'Well, I suppose I could say, thanks be to God for small mercies. But there's part of me says now that since I have to suffer for it I wish I'd made it a three week job. There's another thing, this'll likely have queered me pitch with Jinny. You know you told me to try me hand, well I did, and she had promised to do a show with me next week in Newcastle.'

'Well, this'll test her. Look at it that way: if she can't stand by you in this then to my mind she's not for you.'

'Ah, well, time'll tell, boss. But I want to say thanks for taking the boy in last night. I told him if anything should happen to go to his granny's an' not to bother you; and when it did he told me flatly he wasn't goin' there. Bairns should love their grannies, shouldn't they? And grannies should love their bairns. But still, I never loved me ma nor she me, so what can I expect. God Almighty! It's a funny life.'

'Well, it's got to be lived; and so you get home and change and get back on the job.'

'I'll do that, boss, an' thanks for all you've done an' that comes from the bottom of me heart. It does that, the bottom of me heart.'

'You and your bloody barmy Irish tongue. Go on, get yourself off. . . .'

Bill had hardly drawn the car to a stop outside his office when Peter Honnington hurried towards him, saying, 'Don't get out. Someone rang from your house about ten minutes ago. Your wife's in need of you.'

His stomach turned over; and yet, even as he turned the car around, he thought, of course Honnington wouldn't say she's started, or the bairn's comin'. Oh! what odds. This was it. This was it. Damn the red lights! It was always the way, when you hit one you hit half a dozen. *Come on. Come on. Come on.* How long would she be in labour? A few hours? Some of them took a few days. Oh, my God! That would drive him mad. Not a few days; he'd had enough waitin'. But the time had come. The excitement lifted him off the seat for a moment and he cried at himself, 'Well, get goin'! it's amber.'

He hadn't known what to expect when he arrived at the house. Perhaps Fiona would have been sitting in the hall, her cases ready. Instead, there was Nell, asking, 'How did it go with Davey?'

'Never mind, how did it go with Davey? Where is she? Why isn't she here? I mean, she should be on her way.'

'Well, if she had wings she would fly, but even so she wouldn't fly until she thought it was time. She's in the sitting-room. And don't barge in, Bill Bailey, walk. It'll come in its own time.'

'Have you phoned the hospital, woman?'

'Yes; the hospital has been informed, sir. Your wife is all ready and waiting and she is quite calm. And don't you disturb it.' The last was a hoarse whisper; and now he whispered back at her, 'One of these days I'll tell you what I think about you.'

'That'll be nice.'

'Oh, hello, dear,' said Fiona; 'you haven't been long.'

'Has it started? The pains?'

'Oh, yes, yes. Now for goodness sake, Bill, take that look off your face. Thousands of babies are born every day. I bet you there's a hundred women in this town this very minute waiting for the next spasm.'

'For God's sake Fiona, don't take that attitude. You know how I feel.'

'Yes, yes, I do, dear. Come and sit down.'

'But shouldn't you be on your way?'

'Yes. And I'll go in a minute; I just want to time its next effort.'

She hadn't long to wait. The next moment she was gripping his hand, her nails digging into his flesh.

Nell came into the room dressed for the road and carrying Fiona's coat, a fur hat, and a scarf.

'Get her into these,' she said, handing the coat to Bill; then together they helped her up from the couch.

When she was dressed and about to leave the room, Fiona

83

turned at the door and looked around her, and she said, 'I like this room. I've always liked it.'

Bill made an impatient sound in his throat but kept his tongue quiet.

In the car, Fiona turned to say to Nell who was sitting in the back seat, 'You did lock the front door?'

'Yes, yes, I did.'

'And bolted the back?'

Nell sighed and said, 'Yes, and I bolted the back, and I put the bars up at the windows!'

'Oh, that reminds me.' Fiona looked at Bill now and asked, 'How did Davey come on?' But she didn't quite hear his answer for she was once again seized by a grinding pain.

When it had passed she sat back gasping, and Bill said, 'You should have got to the hospital before all this started.'

'You don't go to hospital before this starts. If you do they send you back.'

'Well, there's one thing sure,' said Nell now; 'it's taken its time in coming but now it's made up its mind it'll be here before you know where you are.'

It appeared that Fiona's baby was indeed galloping, but obviously not in the right direction, for it was still galloping at four o'clock in the afternoon. And it was then the decision was taken that the child must be brought out. Bill was alone in the waiting-room. He had a white coat over his suit. They had made him put it on hours ago, or was it years? Was this still Tuesday? Was it only twelve o'clock when he had held her hand and talked to her? How many times since had they pressed him aside, then let him go back to her? But now she was in the theatre.

He had wanted to see his child born; but an hour ago he didn't know whether he would be able to stand it or not: as he had watched her tortured body heaving, heave after heave, he swore that never again would he put her through this. Never. Never.

84

And now she was down there and they would have to cut her open to take the child away. It wasn't worth it. It wasn't worth it. He had longed for a child, craved for a child; every day that she had been carrying it he had thought about it. When she was asleep at night he had put his hands on her stomach and counted its heart beats, the heart beats that were part of him, all of him.

When the door opened he jumped round as if he was startled. The nurse came in: her face looked quiet, and so was her voice as she said, 'Your wife's back, Mr Bailey. And . . . and you have a daughter.'

He gulped twice in his throat but still he couldn't speak. The nurse now said, 'Doctor . . . Doctor Wells would like a word with you.'

'How . . . how is she? My wife?'

'She's all right; she's asleep.'

'And . . . and the baby?'

The nurse seemed to hesitate a moment before she said, 'Yes, it is all right.' Then she repeated quickly, 'Doctor Wells would like to have a word with you. He is in his office. Would you come this way?'

There was a spring in his step as he followed her into the corridor, down it, along another one; then she was tapping on the door, and when they were bidden to enter she stepped aside and allowed Bill to pass her. Then she closed the door again.

Doctor Wells was a young man . . . well youngish, not yet forty, Bill would have said.

'Sit down, Mr Bailey,' he said.

Bill sat down and looked across the desk into the fresh-coloured face and waited for he knew not what, only that he should now be standing at Fiona's side holding his child. He forced himself to say, 'You . . . you seem to have something to tell me?'

'Yes. Yes, I have, Mr Bailey, unfortunately.'

My God! My God! What is it? What's he going to tell me? he burst out, 'Fiona! She's not?'

'No, no, no. Your wife is quite all right. Very tired naturally but quite all right.'

'The child, it's not quite all right. Is that it?'

'Healthwise – yes, I should say it is perfectly all right; but . . . well, have you heard of Down's Syndrome, Mr Bailey?'

'Down's what?'

'Down's Syndrome?'

'No, no; I can't say I have.'

'Well, I'd better put it another way. I suppose you have seen what is commonly known as a mongol child?'

His chair scraped back on the parquet floor, but he sat perfectly still for what seemed a long, long time. Then he saw his hands go out and grip the edge of the desk; he saw the knuckles whiten as if he were standing outside himself; he saw his head slowly move forward as if it were going to drop off his body the while his real self was standing apart yelling, 'God Almighty! No! No!' But the man sitting in the chair said, in an oddly quiet voice, 'And my daughter is a. . . .' Even his outside self had to help him to press the word through his lips, 'Mongol?'

The doctor answered, 'It is hard to take at first, but I want you to believe it's no fault of yours or your wife's. This child happens in numerous families. But I can tell you this, in nine cases out of ten, they bring happiness because they exude happiness and love and laughter. Of course it is natural that the first reaction of the parent should be one of shock, even anger, perhaps shame, particularly on the father's side, but from my experience in such cases this turns into a feeling of protectiveness and love. I go as far as to say that these children are born with special love, some kind of gift bestowed on them by the gods.'

The anger against this placid individual, this doctor, was rising in him, threatening to choke him. A special gift from the gods. He glowered at the man, but the doctor was looking down onto the blotting pad and seemed to be tracing his finger in a sort of circle. What the hell did he know? A gift from the gods!

He was on his feet glaring down on the doctor and grinding out through his teeth, 'Stop that bloody prattle, for God's sake! You've just old me that my wife has given birth to a mongol, mentally deficient child into the bargain, and you sit there prattling about gifts of love. What d'you know?'

The doctor too was now on his feet and facing him, and his tone matched Bill's own as he said, 'I know, Mr Bailey, because I am the father of a five-year-old mongol child.'

As Bill stared into the man's face he had a queer feeling that his body was shrinking, as if the fat was suddenly being stripped off it. His head was drooping on his shoulders. He knew he was going to cry and he screamed at himself, 'Hell's flames! Hell's flames! not that,' when a voice penetrated through his whirling thoughts, saying quietly, 'Come along and see her.'

He walked out into the corridor and returned along it, and as he did so he knew he'd never again be the same man who had come down this corridor a few minutes ago.

There were only three babies in the nursery. Two had tubes attached to them; the third one was lying on its side, and a nurse was standing looking down into the cot. She moved away when the doctor approached, and he now turned to Bill and said, 'Lift her up.'

Bill looked down onto the child. The side of its face looked rounded like any ordinary child's face. But he couldn't put his hands out towards it. He muttered thickly. 'I'm . . . I'm not used to babies. I haven't held one.'

The doctor now stooped over the cot and lifted the child up; then held it out to Bill, saying, 'It's a simple process. It just lies across your hands.'

He lifted his arms – it seemed there were weights on them – then he was looking down into his daughter's face, seeing it for the first time. Its eyes were open, its lids were blinking, it looked like a Chinese baby might, or Japanese. The small fist opened and shut; then its arm lifted upwards as if it was trying to reach his chin. This was his daughter. This was what he had longed for, lived for over the past months. Never a day, never a night had passed but his mind had conjured up the picture of when the time would come and he would hold his child. And now the time had come and he was holding his child; and it was an idiot.

No! No! No! Not that! It wouldn't be. No! He recalled his schooldays. There had been a boy in his class who looked like a mongol but he had been bright; and he had grown up to be a man. But this child would grow up to be a woman, who should have been as beautiful as her mother. Oh God! Poor Fiona! How would she take it! What if she didn't take it? What if she couldn't bear it?

'She is perfectly made.' The doctor was taking the child from his arms. 'She is very like my Nanette was, very much the same.'

The nurse stepped towards the cot; and now he was following the doctor out into the corridor again and he was talking quietly, 'Your wife is in a side ward. We'll keep her there until she goes home. She needn't be more than two or three days here; she'll face up to it better at home. You have a family?'

'What? Oh yes. Yes, four.'

'Oh, that's good. We have two others. One older and one younger than Nanette.'

Bill paused in his step. 'Younger? Your wife had a child after?'

'Oh, yes, yes. The other two are very ordinary.'

'They . . . they accepted the other one?'

'Oh, yes; they love her. And she's quite bright. She didn't walk until she was about three, nor really talk until then, but she's never stopped since.' He smiled widely now, adding, 'You'll be surprised at the difference she'll make in your home.'

By God! yes. He'd be surprised all right.

He stopped abruptly and, facing the doctor again, he said, 'About . . . about the mind, I mean the mentality?'

'That differs. Here and there you might find one that is exceptionally bright in some special way; but in the main we find the mental age stays around six or seven or so. Yet ask yourself what that really means; or better still talk to a seven-year-old today: they're thinking clearer than many so-called normal adults.'

The doctor kept talking until he pushed open the side ward door where a nurse was writing on a chart, and after she had clipped it on to the bottom of the bed she moved back as they both approached.

As Bill stood gazing down at Fiona whose face looked very red and sweating, he cried at her voicelessly, I'm sorry lass. I'm sorry, for at this moment he was feeling that he was to blame in giving her the child. She could have done without it. She had three of her own and an adopted one, but she knew how he felt and so she had given him a daughter, and her name was to be Angela. It was a farce. Oh God! It was a farce. Yet that man standing at the other side of the bed, he had experienced the same thing. But that fact didn't help him not one jot; such pain was a private thing, it couldn't be shared. No one else's antidote could act as a salve on it.

The doctor was saying, 'She'll sleep for some hours yet. I would go home if I were you.'

'I would rather stay till she wakes if it's all the same. I . . . I won't be in the way?'

'Oh, you won't be in the way. I was just thinking, you might, well, want to tell the family. You could come back later.'

'Aye, perhaps. But . . . but could I stay the night with her?'

'Yes, yes, of course. I don't see why not. Nurse here' – he turned and smiled at the nurse – 'would provide you with an easy chair, or the night staff will see to you.'

89

'How . . . how long will it be before she wakes? I'd like to be here when she comes to. . . . You understand?'

'Yes, I understand. Well now' – he looked at his watch – 'give her another two hours and a half; she should be round by then. You live in the town, don't you?'

'Yes.'

'Well, that's what I should do: take a run home.'

He wanted to put his hand out and touch Fiona's brow, but he resisted and, turning abruptly from the bed, he nodded at the doctor, saying, 'Thank you. I'll . . . I'll likely see you later.' And with that he went out, and drove to home. . . .

As soon as he got in the door they rushed at him like a small avalanche; and behind them stood Nell and Bert.

'Has it come?'

'How's Mam?'

'What is it?'

'Has it really come?'

'When will we be able to go to the hospital?'

'Dad! Dad! Tell us.'

He waved his hand around them, then said, 'Be quiet a minute. Let me get in.' Then he forced himself to say, 'The baby's come; it's a girl. Your mother's all right. She had to have an operation, and now she's asleep. Now get yourselves away for a minute; I want a bath.'

And Nell said, 'And a meal.'

'No; just a cup of tea, Nell; but I do need a bath. I'm going back.'

Nell stared at him; as did Bert. They watched him throw off his overcoat, scarf and hat onto a chair. Then she cried at the children, 'Go on! Do as your dad says. He'll tell you all about it when he has a minute to himself. Go on now, up in the playroom. That's good kids.'

Slowly they obeyed her; that is with the exception of Mark, and he, following quickly after Bill who was moving

90

towards the sitting-room, touched his arm, saying, 'Mam all right, Dad?'

'Yes. Yes, she's all right, Mark. I'll come up in a minute and tell you all about it.'

The boy walked away, a puzzled look on his face, leaving Bill to walk slowly into the sitting-room followed by Nell and Bert. And it was Nell who asked immediately, 'Something gone wrong?'

'You could say that, Nell. Aye, you could say that.'

'Fiona. She's all right?'

'Oh, yes, yes. She had to have a caesarean, but she's all right. I left her sleeping. But I'm going back in a couple of hours time, staying the night.'

'Well, what is it? The baby?'

Bill dropped onto the couch, lay back and put his hand over his eyes before he said, 'Yes, Nell, the baby.'

'Oh my God! Deformed?'

'No, not in that way, Nell, not in that way. Have you heard of Down's Syndrome?' He was sitting up now looking from her to Bert. And he watched them glance at each other before Nell said, 'Yes.' Then, 'Oh no! No, Bill. And Fiona . . . how did she take it?'

'She doesn't know yet. She hasn't come round.'

'No, no: of course not.' Nell dropped into a chair. 'Is . . . is it bad?'

'What d'you mean, is it bad?'

'Well, they look like. . . .'

'Yes, it looks a bit like a Chinese, but otherwise it's all right. As the doctor said, perfectly formed.'

'I'm sorry.'

Bill now looked at Bert, saying, 'So am I, Bert. So am I. But there you are. As the doctor said, it happens to all kinds of couples.' And he added on a derisive laugh, 'And he put it over very well, as if he was selling something, that these kind of bairns often bring happiness into a home. Anyway, he should know, he's got one.'

91

'The doctor's got one?'

Bill nodded at Nell, saying, 'Yes, a five-year-old; and he says she's lovely, or words to that effect. But I would have voted for one as ugly as sin itself as long as it was normal. Oh God! How Fiona's goin' to take it, I don't know; that's if she takes it at all. . . .Give me a large whisky there, Bert, will you?'

Bert, the staunch teetotaller, went to the drinks cabinet in the corner of the room and poured out what he imagined would be a double whisky. And as he handed it to Bill he said, 'God works in strange ways His miracles to perform.'

'Aw, Bert! God in Heaven or whatever, don't come religion on me at this time. If you're so much in contact with Him then you ask Him why. Aye, that's it.' His voice was rising now. 'Ask Him why.' He put his glass to his lips and threw off half the whisky, then coughed and choked on it. And leaning back against the couch again, he muttered, 'I'm sorry. I'm sorry.'

'It's all right, boss; but I've seen these bairns. I've got one in my Sunday School class. And a nicer lad you couldn't meet. And he's not mental. He's nine years old and for his type is bright.'

'There you've said it, Bert, there you've said it, for his type.'

'Well, I'll tell you this much, boss. I've got twenty-eight children, when they all come, and they're all supposed to be normal except Roger. But let me tell you, Roger is more intelligent than at least half of them. The only thing noticeable about him, apart from his eyes, is that he's got a sort of slight lisp. But I can tell you he's all there. And he's got three brothers and two sisters and I wouldn't swap him for the top two brothers I can tell you that. Now I don't know how your little girl will turn out but all I can say is, give her a chance. And I will say this, whether it vexes you or pleases you, boss, there's nothing happens in this world that can't be laid at the door of man, right from the beginning of time, through Christ's Crucifixion, wars and massacres; and the only hope of relief is through belief in God. But that of course is only my opinion, and I don't often voice it, as Nell knows, 'cos I'm afraid it isn't hers, not totally. Anyway, boss, what about the bairns? Are you goin' to tell them?'

Bill now looked from Bert to Nell, and he shook his head as he said, 'I don't think I can. Not tonight anyway.'

'Would . . . would you like me to do it, Bill?'

'Would you, Nell?'

'Bert and I . . . we'll do it together.'

Bill now finished the last of the whisky and, handing the glass to Bert, he rose from the couch and went out. . . .

He was in the bathroom when Nell and Bert went upstairs and into the playroom. And on their entry Mamie jumped from the couch, crying, 'Have we got a new baby?'

'Yes, dear, yes, we've got a new baby. It's a girl.' She looked at the other three. There was no excitement on their faces. It was Katie now who spoke: 'Something not right, is it, Nell?' she said. 'Is it Mam?'

'No, no, dear; your mother's all right. Come and sit down.'

Not until they were all seated did she glance at Bert, and it was he who started. Looking from one to the other, he said, 'You all love your Mam and Dad, don't you?' None of the children spoke, but Mark and Katie exchanged a puzzled look, then waited. And Bert went on: 'Well, I know it goes without saying that you do. Now in the future they're goin' to need all your love and co-operation because of the baby.'

'Something wrong with it?'

Bert looked at Willie, and he said, 'In a way.'

In the stunned silence that fell on the children Nell now said, 'There's a thing called Down's Syndrome. You won't have heard of it, but it's when a baby's face is slightly distorted. I know you've seen children like it in the street.'

There was a thin whisper now from Mark as he said, 'You mean mongol children?'

'Yes mongol children.'

'And that's what Mam's got?'

There was a trace of horror in Katie's voice, and Nell said, 'Yes, that's what your mam's got. Now what you've all got to remember is that the baby is your sister. And I was going to say that you will have to love her; but you will find, from my experience and those who know more about it than me, and Bert is one of them, that these children give out love and affection. That's all they seem to live for, to give out love and affection. They are not aware that they are different from other children. There is a simplicity about them.'

'Do . . . do they go mad?'

'No, Willie.' Both Nell and Bert answered together; then Nell went on, 'Of course not.'

'He didn't mean mad, Nell . . . well, he meant just mental, like those in the school at Burrows Road.'

Nell paused a moment because she was about to say, 'Not necessarily,' but instead she was emphatic and said, 'Not at all. The only thing is I understand they don't grow into adults. Well, yes, of course they grow up, but what I mean is their minds won't expand any further than, say, Willie's is now. And he's bright enough, isn't he?' She smiled from one to the other. 'Too bright at times. Anyway, there it is. Now, naturally your dad is upset and is going back to the hospital to be there when your mam wakes up, and it's only natural that she too will be upset. So, when she brings the baby home you'll all have to pull together to help her accept the situation.'

'People will talk.'

'What d'you mean?' said Nell, now looking at Katie.

'Well, they talk about that boy round the corner in Saville Street.'

'You mean John Bent?'

'I . . . I don't know what his name is, but his legs and arms and head are all over the place.'

'Yes, they might be. But his brain inside his head is not all over the place, Katie. He's very bright. In fact, he's as bright as any man. And if you're going to be afraid of what people will say, then it's a bad look out for this family. And I'll be ashamed of the lot of you.'

'It's come as a surprise, Nell.'

It was Bert who answered Mark, saying, 'Yes, naturally, Mark, it's come as a surprise, and to all of us. But the ones who are goin' to feel it most are your mam and dad, and they'll want support. That's what Nell's saying, they'll need your support every inch of the way, at least at first. Now we are going downstairs to get your dad a drink and to try to get him to eat a bite. And try to understand if he doesn't come in and see you the night because . . . well, he's in a bit of a state and worried about your mam. You understand?'

He got to his feet, and Nell too rose, and she said, 'Get ready for bed. I'll be up shortly. And another thing, your dad will be staying at the hospital all night with your mam. But don't worry, Bert and I will be here.'

As they made their way downstairs Nell said under her breath, 'Thank God that's over.'

Fiona was still asleep when Bill reached the hospital. And he noted there was already a big easy chair placed by the side of the bed. The day staff were leaving and the night staff coming on. Two nurses came in, nodded at him and smiled, then set up an apparatus on top of the locker, from which they attached something to Fiona's arm. Then one of them explained, 'This will take her blood pressure during the night, save disturbing her. Make yourself comfortable. Would you like a cup of tea?'

'I wouldn't mind. Thank you.'

'Do you take sugar?'

'No. No thanks, no sugar.'

The tea was weak but hot. He sipped at it, while all the time looking at Fiona. . . .

Half an hour later she made restless moaning sounds, then opened her eyes and, seeing him, she said, 'Oh, Bill. Bill.'

'It's all right, love. It's all right.'

'The baby?'

'She's all right an' all.'

'A girl?'

'Aye, a girl.'

'Oh, Bill. . . .It was tough going to . . . towards the end.'

'Yes, dear, very tough going. It's over.'

She drew in a long breath, then said, 'I'm so tired, I feel I could sleep for a week.'

'You go to sleep then, dear. You go to sleep.'

'But . . . but I'd like to see her.'

'You will in the morning. She's asleep too now. D'you know what time it is?'

'No.'

'Going on for ten o'clock.'

'Ten o'clock. Have . . . have you been here all the time?'

'Yes, except when I slipped home.'

'To tell them?'

'Yes, to tell them.'

'I . . . I bet they were excited.'

'Yes, they were. They were.'

'Oh, Bill. I'm . . . I'm glad for you.'

She closed her eyes, turned her head to the side and he realised with some surprise that she had gone to sleep. . . .

What time he himself fell asleep he naturally didn't know, but he had strange dreams. And when he finally awoke it was to the sound of cups rattling and the feeling of bustle around him. He didn't open his eyes because he still felt very tired. It came into his consciousness that he had a slight cramp in his right leg. He pushed out his heel and brought his toes up until the pain went. Then he heaved a sigh and opened his eyes and looked on the smiling face of Fiona. She was sitting propped up in bed drinking a cup of tea. She smiled at him and in quite a casual voice, said, 'Feel better, Mr Bailey?' then added, 'There's a cup of tea to your hand. Drink that, and then you'll be able to see me clearly.'

He put out a groping hand, picked up the cup and almost drained it with one go; then, pulling himself forward to the end of the chair, he leant an elbow on the bedside and put his other hand up to her face and stroked her cheek, saying, 'How d'you feel?'

'Fine. Excited. Raring to go. The nurse tells me I'll be here for a day or two; but still, what odds.' She brought her head down to his, saying softly now, 'I'm dying to see her. Apparently they have rules and regulations, and she's sound asleep.'

When he bowed his head she said softly, 'Bill. What's the matter? Look at me, Bill.'

When he looked up she said again, 'What's the matter? Something's wrong. She's not . . .? No, no, no. She's not deformed or anything like . . .?'

He gripped both her hands as he brought his words out hesitantly: 'No, not what you call deformed.'

'What d'you mean?' – she pulled herself back from him – 'Not what I'd call deformed. What d'you mean? Tell me.'

'Quiet. Quiet.' He looked towards the door, then said, 'Now, dear . . . my very, very, dear, there's something you've got to know. It's goin' to come as a shock as it did to me, but . . . but we've got to live with it.'

She pressed her head back tight against the pillows. 'She . . . she is deformed! She's . . . she's not right! She's. . . .'

'She isn't deformed, and as far as it goes she's all right, but – I'm sure you will have heard the term, I hadn't – but she's what you call a Down's Syndrome baby.'

Her eyes slowly closed while her mouth opened wide as if to emit a scream, and he said sharply, 'Fiona! Fiona! Please!'

'No! No!' She was now shaking her head on the pillow in deep denial, and again, 'No! No! All these months I never, never felt so contented in my life. She . . . she can't be. She can't. They would have told me.'

'Remember, love, remember you wouldn't go to the clinics. You said you felt so well you wanted none of it. When you did go it was too late, much too late.'

Her head came up from the pillow and her face was hanging over his as she said through clenched teeth, 'I won't have it, I won't. It can't happen to us. I wanted her for you, just for you. I couldn't give you a . . . a mongol, because that's what you're telling me, isn't it? It's a mongol. I won't have it! I won't have her. I won't! I won't!'

He pushed himself back and stood up, causing her to drop onto the pillow again and her mouth to open when he said as harshly: 'Fiona! You've got to have it. We've both got to have it.'

Through a whimper now, she said, 'I don't have to. I've got three healthy children. I don't have to.'

Bending over her now and his hands on her shoulders, he said grimly, 'You haven't only got three children, you've got four children of your own.'

'NO!' It was a shout, and the door opened and a passing nurse came in, saying, 'Is . . . is everything all right?'

Bill straightened up from the bed. 'No!' he answered the nurse; 'everything isn't all right. Would you mind bringing the baby?'

'Now?'

'Yes, now.'

'I'll see sister.'

'Do that, and quickly. Please.'

Fiona's eyes were still closed but she was talking quietly now: 'It's no good, Bill, I just couldn't. I have seen such children and I just couldn't.'

He said nothing, just stood looking grimly down on her, listening to her protestations, unintelligible mutterings now.

It was a full ten minutes before the door opened and the sister came in, saying brightly, 'Good-morning!'

'Good-morning.' Bill nodded at her.

Fiona still lay with her eyes closed.

The sister now stood by the side of the bed, saying, 'Mrs Bailey, here is your baby.' There was no compromise in the voice; it was a definite statement.

In answer, Fiona turned her head to the side, but in a moment Bill was round the bed, and he almost grabbed the child from the sister's arms, his action thrusting her aside.

'Take the child!'

'I . . . I've told you, Bill.'

'No matter what you've told me, you've got a baby to see to. Take her!'

When there was no response and her body moved, as if painfully, away from him, he was round to the other side of the bed again in a flash. And now he thrust the child down into her stiff arms; and it was only a reflex action that made her bring her hands up to stop it from rolling onto the bed.

It was as if her head and neck had been out of use for years, so slowly and so painfully did it turn. And then her eyes were forced to look down on her daughter and what she saw were two bright eyes looking up at her, a little face that had a suspicion of a smile on it, and fingers that were clasping in and out. And when, as with Bill, the arm came up and the hand seemed to be aiming to touch the face above it, Fiona pressed her head away. But she continued to stare at the child. It had a tuft of light brown hair on the top of its head.

She couldn't bear it. Why? Why? She was normal. Bill was normal. Her mother and father had been normal. Bill's father was normal. Why? Why? As she went to thrust the child away Bill's hands grabbed it from her, and now he was holding it tight against his chest. And he startled the sister, but not Fiona because she was used to his voice, by bawling,

'All right! All right! You won't have her, but she is mine. *My daughter*. My responsibility. And her needs will come first. D'you hear? So, if that's how you want it, that's how it's going to be.'

5

Five days later Bill brought the child home. And it *was* Bill who brought her home, because he carried her from the hospital to the car, placed her carefully on the back seat, then drove her and her mother to the house. And it was he who picked up the child, carried it in and straight upstairs to the small nursery that had been made by taking down a partition between the boxroom and the airing cupboard. And there the children had crushed in and around it.

Sammy Love happened to be present at the time, and when no comments came from any of the children it was he who looked up at Bill and, smiling, he said, 'She's canny.' And Bill, with a large lump in his throat, looked down on the boy, put his hand on his head and said, 'Yes, Sammy, she's canny.'

A short while later, when Bill stood in the kitchen with Nell, he thumped his fist against the framework of the sink as he said, 'This is going to be hell! She'll never accept it. What are we going to do, Nell?'

'Give her time. I can understand how she feels. She wanted to give you something. Most of her feeling is one of guilt, not so much against the child but somehow feeling she's let you down. I'm sure that's at the bottom of it. Who knows, she may end up being a blessing in disguise.'

He rounded on her now, crying, 'For God's sake! Nell, don't come that tack. I've heard it so often these last few days. But I know, too, of such bairns who aren't a blessing in disguise.'

'Well,' Nell came back at him harshly, 'can you show me any normal family and the parents pointing to a child and saying, they're a blessing in disguise? No; I know of people who wish their normal offspring had never been born. Anyway, she'll have to accept her in the end. Other mothers have, and they've probably been saddled with just the one. She's got plenty of support all round her; she'll just have to pull herself together. But then' – her voice dropped – 'it'll take time. And I'll say to you, Bill, go canny with her; she's had a shock. And oh, I know, you've had one an' all. I'll never forget the night you came back from the hospital after seeing her for the first time. I wouldn't have been surprised if you had thrown her off then. Anyway, pray God that something will happen to make Fiona change her mind.' She laughed. 'I'm getting as bad as Bert, aren't I, calling on the Deity every possible occasion.'

Nell was to say later, the Deity must have heard because something did happen to change Fiona's mind.

Mrs Vidler had stayed well over a month in America. She had written a short note to Fiona to say her friends were pressing her to extend her holiday – these were her words – and she would let her know when she was coming home.

But she didn't let her know until after she had actually arrived. It was the week before Christmas on the Friday afternoon, the nineteenth to be exact. Nell had just gone to pick up Katie and Mamie from school. Fiona had the house to herself except for the child, and it was in the nursery where it remained most of the time except when either Bill

102

or Nell brought it downstairs or the children carried it into the playroom. Fiona wouldn't let the thought penetrate her mind that it was strange how her children had taken to the child, even vying with each other to hold it.

She was about to enter the kitchen when the phone rang; and so she returned to the hall, picked it up and in a flat voice said the number, but before she had finished she heard her mother say, 'Fiona.'

'Oh . . . yes, Mother. Where are you?'

'I'm home, of course.'

'You . . . you said you were going to let me know.'

'Well, I didn't, and I'm home.'

'What's the matter? You sound. . . .'

'Yes, I know how I sound. I want to talk to you. Can you come round?'

'I'm sorry, I can't, Mother.'

'Why?'

'I'm alone in the house but for the' – she paused – 'the baby.'

'Oh yes, the baby. You say you are alone?'

'Yes.'

'I'll come straight round then.' The phone clicked down.

Fiona turned; stood still for a moment, then went into the sitting-room. She had always said she loved this room, but not any more because there was no happiness in it now. There was no happiness in the house. It was a divided house: Bill and the children on one side, Nell and Bert somewhere in the middle, and Sammy Love . . . where was Sammy Love? When he was with her he was for her, when he was with the child he was very much for the child. . . .

It almost seemed that her mother had been standing outside the door, and when the bell rang twice she wanted to cry out, 'All right! All right! I'm coming,' but when she opened the door and saw the person standing on the step who spoke like her mother but wasn't her mother, yet was, she stood aside and allowed her to enter.

'Don't stare at me like that.'

'What do you expect me to do?' The woman before her was dressed, not as she usually was in good class but plain clothes, but in a flamboyant imitation fur coat with an enormous collar and cuffs and a woollen hat on top of her russet-coloured hair, which when Fiona had last seen it had been a light brown streaked with grey. But then there was her face: there was a tightness at the corner of the eyes, very like – Fiona could not make herself even think, the child's – and the droop and lines from each side of the mouth had gone. Her face had the appearance of one that had just been taken out of a mudpack, smooth and unlined but ready to slip back into its natural slackness once the astringent wore off. But in her mother's case the astringent wouldn't wear off. *She'd had her face lifted.*

'Yes. Yes, you can look, and you can say it: why did you have to go all the way to America to have it done?' They were going towards the sitting-room now. 'Because I understood they did a better job there, and they have.'

'Then why are you in a temper? You should be pleased with yourself.'

'It's . . . it's him, Davey. I couldn't believe it.'

'What's he done? Sit down. Sit down.'

In the presence of her mother's agitation Fiona felt calm for the first time in weeks. Mrs Vidler, seated now on the couch, her open coat showing that she was wearing a tight fitting red woollen dress which, in its turn, showed that she had certainly lost pounds in weight, was clasping and unclasping her hands as she said, 'I . . . I did it just for him because . . . well, he gave me the impression that he was interested. But I went straight round there and what do I find? He's got a *woman* installed.'

'Well, he's a young man. He looked upon you as a mother.'

'*He did not, Fiona.* He encouraged me.'

'I don't know about encouraging you, Mother, I do know

that you threw yourself at him. But even then he saw you as a motherly figure.'

'I am no motherly figure.' And she wagged her head as she said this. 'All that way, the dreadful journey and all the expense . . . yes, the expense. I'll tell him. I will.'

'I wouldn't if I were you, Mother; I would save what little dignity you have left; and I'd also get out of those awful clothes and be yourself.'

'I'll . . . I'll never be myself again. And . . . and I hate America.'

'I thought it was lovely and the people were marvellous.'

'Yes, as long as you're spending money. Oh' – she got to her feet and began to walk up and down – 'why had this to happen to me, at my age?'

'There you said it, Mother, at your age.'

Now her mother rounded on her; 'And may I ask what's the matter with you? Not a kind word out of you, not a word of welcome. Are you ill? You look it. Is it this post-natal depression that all mothers seem to indulge in these days?'

'No, I'm not suffering from post-natal depression, Mother. And I'm being as thoughtful of you as you are of me.'

'Here we go again. Anyway, may I ask what the latest effort is? Am I a grandmother to a boy or a girl?'

'It's a girl.'

'Well, where is she?'

'In the nursery.'

'You've got a nursery now?'

'We've made a makeshift one. Would you like to come up and see her?'

'Well, it's the least I can do, isn't it?'

'Yes, Mother; it's the least you can do. . . .'

The room held a cot, a small table, a cupboard and two straight-backed chairs. The child was awake and gurgling; they both heard it as they opened the door. There was a permanent night-light glowing as the only other light in the room was from a fanlight in the roof. Fiona switched on the main light; then one at each side of the cot, they stood looking down on the gurgling child.

'*Dear God!*' It was a thin whisper from Mrs Vidler. 'It's a. . . .'

'Yes, Mother, a mongol.'

'*Oh, my goodness!*' Oh, really! How on earth could this happen to you? Are . . . are you going to keep it?'

'Yes, Mother, we are going to keep it. And it isn't an "it", it's a "she".'

'They . . . they grow up mental.'

'They do nothing of the sort, Mother!' It was a bawl that would have done credit to Bill, and Mrs Vidler reared up and said, 'Don't you dare shout at me like that! Anyway, what do you expect from that man? There's nothing like this on our side of the family; it's through him.'

'It isn't through him, Mother. These things happen to all types of people.'

'It's genes; it's passed down.'

'It isn't genes, and it is not passed down.'

'All right, all right, it is not passed down; but this has come about through him, and what will people say?'

'I don't give a damn about what people say, Mother.'

'Well, you should. And don't expect me to be grand-mother to it. There are homes for such children.'

'Yes, there are, Mother; and this is the home for this child, my child, Bill's child.' Of a sudden her arms went out and grabbed the baby from the cot, and she pulled it to her breast and, holding it tightly there, she said, 'And what is more, I'll put her in the pram and take her outside, and everybody I meet I'll tell them that Mrs Vidler is my mother.'

'Stop it, Fiona. Stop it!'

'No; you stop it, Mother. And get out! Do you hear? Get out!'

She was yelling at the top of her voice now; and her mother had already backed towards the door and onto the landing. And the noise must have been heard in the kitchen, for from there emerged Nell, Katie, and Mamie; and Nell could only briefly notice the change in Mrs Vidler because she was staring up at Fiona coming down the stairs, screaming at the top of her voice as she held the child to her, 'And don't come back into this house until you're asked. Do you hear? And I hope you find a man who will appreciate your face-lift and all the money you've spent on it. As for Davey Love, he looked on you as a grannie, not even a mother.'

'Fiona! Fiona!'

'Mam! Mam!'

Nell was holding Fiona by the shoulders now and Katie was gripping her mother's arm while Mamie, her face twisting into tears, was tugging at her dress.

'She's gone. She's gone. Come on. Come on into the sitting-room. Sit down.'

'Nell . . . Nell . . . she said. . . .'

'It doesn't matter what she said, dear. Give me the child here.'

'No, no; I want it. It's Bill's. It's mine. It's Bill's.'

'Don't cry. Don't cry, dear.'

'I must cry, Nell, I must cry. I've been wicked, wicked. Poor Bill. It's Bill's. It's mine.'

As her crying mounted she pressed the child tighter to her and began to rock it, and Nell, turning to Katie, whispered, 'Go and ring the yard. Ask your dad to come home. Quick!'

When Katie got through and heard Bill's voice, she said, 'Dad.'

'Yes. Who's that?'

'It's Katie.'

'Oh, yes. What's the matter?'

'Dad, can you come home; it's Mam.'

'What's happened? What's she done?'

'She's . . . she's done nothing, Dad. Gran's been here. She's upset; but I think it's a good upset.'

107

'A good upset? What d'you mean?'

'I can't explain. Just come, Dad.'

Katie could hear her mother's cries and they were mingled with Mamie's; and then Nell's voice, saying, 'It's all right, dear, it's all right. Don't hold the baby so tight. Just rock it. Just nurse it. That's right, that's right.'

'Nell. I hate her. I hate her.'

'Yes, I know, dear. Very few people like her.'

'It's wrong to hate, Nell. It's wrong to hate.'

'Here! let me dry your eyes. Try to stop crying, dear.'

'I want to go on crying, Nell; I want to cry forever. I've been wicked. Poor Bill. I'll not put her in a home, ever! I'll not put her in a home.'

'No, of course you won't; we wouldn't let you even if you wanted to; we all love her.'

'Yes, you all love her. I didn't love her, but you all loved her, Bill most of all. But it wasn't love really, not really. It was compassion. Yes, that's it, compassion, compassion.'

'It's all right, dear. It's all over.'

'No, no, Nell; it's not all over, it's only starting. Don't take her from me. No, don't take her from me. I won't hurt her. I'll hold her like this and rock her. My mind's been going round in circles, Nell; I don't know where I've been. My mother has been in me. I'm part of her you know. Yes, I am, I am. And I've been seeing Angela through her eyes. I'm glad she came. And she doesn't look younger, she looks awful. Her face matches her character, tight, stretched, selfish. Can a face be selfish? It's all right, Nell, it's all right; I'm not hurting her, I'm just rocking her.'

'Lie back, dear. Lie back. Try to relax.'

'Sammy said I would get a surprise. Sammy comes out with odd things and they always mean something. He's an odd boy, that, is Sammy. Oh! Nell, Nell; I think I'm going to die.'

'No, you're not going to die, dear. You're going to live and make us all happy again.'

108

'Bill will never be happy again.'

'Oh yes, he will. Once he sees you holding her, he'll be happy.'

'Will he, Nell? I'm so tired, Nell, so very tired. I've been fighting inside me all the time, wanting to touch her, because she isn't bad to look at, is she?'

'No, no; she's not. We all think she's sweet.'

'Well I wouldn't say she's sweet, but she's not bad.'

She had a bout of coughing and choking, but still she would not relinquish the child.

And five minutes later she was still holding it, still rocking it, and still crying when Bill entered the room. He paused for a moment, then hurried to the couch and sat down beside her, saying, 'Aw! love, that's it: cry. That's it: cry.'

'I'm sorry, Bill, I'm sorry.'

'You've nothing to be sorry for, hinny. Nothing. Nothing. From now on everything will be all right. There now. There now.'

When the front door bell rang, Katie ran to open it, and she greeted the man on the step: 'Oh, hello, Mr Meredith. Come in. Come in.'

'What's the matter, Katie? Why are you crying?'

'It's Mam. She's . . . she's come round.'

'Come round from what?'

'The baby.'

'Oh, has it come? I've been in Scotland you know; Sir Charles's brother died. I . . . I went to the funeral.'

'Oh, I'm sorry. I mean about Sir Charles's brother. Give me your coat.'

'Mr Meredith.'

'Yes, Katie?'

'Don't . . . don't look surprised when you see the baby, will you not?'

'Should I?'

'You might.'

'All right, Katie; I won't look surprised.'

When he entered the sitting-room and saw the situation he continued walking slowly forward, and Bill turned to him, saying, 'Oh, hello there. You've got back then.'

'Yes, I got back this morning. I thought I'd look in. So it's arrived.'

'Yes, Rupert, it's arrived.' Bill nodded towards him. 'Show Rupert our daughter, Fiona.'

'Hello, Rupert.' Fiona could hardly see him through the still running tears. And he said, 'Hello, Fiona.' Then he looked down on the child and he smiled: 'What's her name?' he asked.

'Angela.'

He glanced at Bill and repeated, 'Angela? Well, she'll likely turn out to be an angel in disguise.'

Nell rose from the other side of the couch, saying, 'Well, I think we could all do with a cup of tea. And then you Katie, and you Mamie, and the rest of the gang can get down to those Christmas decorations and rake out the things from the garret for the tree. Are you going to Scotland for the Christmas, Mr Meredith?'

'No, Nell. I've just come back from there. Sir Charles and Lady Kingdom are staying over the holidays. But coming down in the train, I was thinking that as I am a very lone man there might be a nice family who would invite me to stay over the Christmas holidays.'

Katie made a sound between a giggle and a sniff, and Bill said, 'You're welcome. More than welcome. But this'll be your bed.' He thumbed towards the couch.

'It will suit me.'

'This house will soon be bursting at the seams.' Nell went out smiling now. And Bill, looking at Fiona who was lying back taking in deep gasping breaths, the child still held, but gently now, in her arms, said, 'That reminds me. I've got a Christmas box for you.'

She looked up at him but said nothing.

'Tomorrow I'm goin' to take you to see it: in fact, I'll take

110

the whole squad of you because I want more than one opinion.' He turned to Rupert, saying, 'D'you know Burnstead Mere House?'

'Oh, yes, yes. It's a lovely place. Beautiful gardens too. And the mere is quite a large one. I've been there. You after that?'

'Yes. It's got twelve main rooms and a small indoor pool. What d'you think about that?' He was now putting his face close to Fiona's.

'If you think it's for us, then it's for us. Wipe my face, will you?'

As Bill gently wiped Fiona's face, Rupert caught hold of Mamie's hand and took her from the room. But in the kitchen, before he had time to say anything, Mamie cried, not only to Nell and Katie, but to Mark, Willie, and Sammy, who had just come in and were now all bright faced. 'We're going to move into a big house, like a palace, with twelve rooms and a swimming pool, and a river at the bottom.'

The announcement seemed to still them all and to cause them to look at Rupert as if for confirmation or further enlightenment. And it was Nell who said, 'Is that a fact?'

'It would seem so, Nell. It's Bill's Christmas box to Fiona, and to you all, I should say.'

'Oh, well. Anyway' – Nell shook her head – 'she's already given him his Christmas box.' Then turning to the children, she added, 'Now gang, let's get going. Away to your posts, all of you, and prepare for a happy Christmas. And believe me I never thought we should see it. But thanks to your dear sweet grandmama, she has worked a small miracle. And as my husband says, they do happen.'

111

6

They couldn't be taken to see the house the next day for the people were moving out. So it was the day before Christmas Eve when the whole family piled into the two cars, the second driven by Rupert, who took Mark and Willie, and, of course it went without saying, Sammy Love. Nell, Katie and Mamie were seated in the back of Bill's car, with the baby, wrapped in two large shawls, a bonnet and woolly boots, being nursed by Katie.

'You all right, dear?'

'Yes, Bill.' Fiona nodded at him.

'Warm enough?'

'Yes. Yes, I couldn't help but be in this.' She hugged around her the sheepskin coat with which he had surprised her only yesterday. Then she said, 'How far is it?'

'Oh, about half an hour's run, a bit more perhaps. You all right back there?'

'Fine.' The concerted answer came from the three of them. 'But,' Nell added, 'we will feel better when you get a move on, if this machine works. My old banger would have been away by now.'

'Yes, making for the scrap-yard.'

'Don't you dare insult Maria!' And the laughter this brought about seemed to create the atmosphere for further backchat during the journey in the back seat. In the main, however, Fiona sat quiet, because she felt quiet. The only description she could give to herself with regard to the change in her since that dreadful crying bout was that she was experiencing a kind of silence. Everything she had thought over the last few days seemed to have dropped into this silence and melted away. She didn't know if she liked this feeling or not. But what she did know was that she was thankful unto God that things were right between her and Bill again, and that her mind had accepted the child even while, as yet, her heart was not touched. And yet there were times when she looked at it and it looked back at her she experienced the very feeling that it was trying to tell her something, and also that there was something bigger in life itself encased in that small body, and struggling to get out. She had told herself that this was mere fancy, a tangent of that feeling she had had before her outburst that she would likely go out of her mind, and end up in the same place as Rupert's fiancée. Nevertheless, it was strange how, since that outburst, the atmosphere in the house had done a complete somersault: everyone now seemed happy, and the child was the focus of it. It seemed as if the child was going to alter all their lives. No, not seemed, it had already done so.

Nell was saying, 'And who d'you think's going to clean this twelve-roomed house of yours, Mr Bailey?'

'Well, what d'you think I pay you for? And there's not only twelve rooms, I forgot to tell you there's a granny annexe an' all. I thought it would do for Mrs Vidler.'

There were indecipherable noises from the back, while Fiona said, 'Yes, yes, it could, dear.'

'Over your dead body! Anyway she's not a granny any more is she? My God! that face. You know, it's funny about faces: those clever bods can't alter expressions in the eyes,

113

and it's the eyes that give away age, more than wrinkled skin.'

A short while later Bill got out of the car and, taking the keys from his pocket, he unlocked a pair of iron gates, pushed them wide, then took his seat again before driving through a short avenue of trees and onto a broad sweep of pink tarmac, fronting a long two-storeyed house showing three dormer windows in the roof, and a stone pillared porch covering the front door.

With another key, Bill unlocked the heavy oak door and, pushing this wide too, he said, 'Enter Mrs Bailey and family.' Then looking over his shoulder, he said, 'Here are the rest.'

When Rupert and the three boys stepped into the hall there was silence among them all for a moment. Then it was Katie who said, in a very small voice, 'You said they had moved, Dad. But look, there's the carpets and curtains and. . . .'

'They go with the house, Katie; and one or two other things an' all, bits of big furniture here and there 'cos they're movin' into a smaller place. There was only the two of them, their family were grown up and gone.'

Following Bill, they now walked towards one of the doors at the far end of the hall, and as he pushed it open he said, 'What d'you think of that?'

No one spoke till Fiona said, 'It's a beautiful room.'

'And you've seen nothing yet, Mrs B.'

And they certainly hadn't seen anything yet. The dining-room brought gasps from them because the dining-table and chairs were still there, also a sideboard and a large leather suite.

What was called the study was, to them, more like a small library, with bookshelves covering two walls as well as a huge break-front bookcase.

It was Rupert who said, 'If I remember rightly there was a billiard room somewhere, Bill.'

'Aye; it used to be a billiard room, but now it's a kind of

114

games room with exercise machines and God knows what.'

'Where? Where?'

Both Willie and Mark made for the door, and when Bill cried at them, 'Hold your hand a minute! Keep with the party or else you might get lost. When I've shown you the lay-out, then you may go mad.'

The games room brought oohs! and aahs! from all the children; but it was the kitchen that brought the oohs! and aahs! from both Fiona and Nell. 'It's something you would dream of,' said Nell. 'Look at the size of this fridge. My! it'll take some filling. And the dishwasher. Oh! Fiona, look.' She had walked through another door. 'The utility room is nearly as big as our house. Oh, I wish Bert was here; it might give him some ideas to build on at the back of our place; you can hardly get into the kitchen.'

Another door led to two smaller rooms, and when Fiona asked Bill what they would have been used for, he, glancing at Rupert and putting on what he imagined to be his voice, said, 'The servants, my dear. The servants,' whereupon everyone laughed again and repeated, 'Oh, yes; the servants, my dear. The servants,' while Rupert, not to be outdone and assuming a tone that he imagined was Bill's, said, 'Well, boss, I wouldn't mind 'avin' 'em. I can buttle.'

'You can what?' Katie was now hanging onto his arm.

'Buttle, miss. Buttle. Be a butler.'

'Well, who knows; we could take you on at that.' Bill was leading them along a corridor now and so into a separate apartment whic consisted of a good-sized sitting-room, a bedroom, a kitchen, and a bathroom. And Katie was now crying, 'Oh, I could live in this end, and have it all to myself. And look!' She was pointing through a glass door. 'It's got a covered patio and a garden.'

It was when, a few minutes later, they went into the pool room that they all became speechless for a moment. The water looked deep blue; the bath itself was tiled: the bottom blue, and the sides white. At the near end of the pool was a set of steps in half-moon Roman fashion leading down to the water. At the far end was a diving board. Except for the near end, there was a supporting rail all round at water level. And to the side, there were two dressing-rooms.

'Tain't true, is it?'

They all glanced at Sammy. He was looking up at Bill; and Bill, returning his glance, said, ''Tis true, Sammy. It was a dream, a dream of a lifetime, but it's come true. If you dream hard enough for something it'll come true in the end.'

'Are there other people after it, Dad?' Mark's question was quiet yet showing a little apprehension. Bill pursed his lips and said, 'Aye; yes, there's other people after it; but there's one obstacle, it's the price. Now come on, come on, you've seen nothing yet.'

And how true, Fiona thought as they 'toured' the bedrooms: with three of them having a bathroom en suite, as it was called. There were two other bathrooms. These they found along another corridor where the other three bedrooms were. All the bedrooms were carpeted and curtained, and in two of the main ones the beds remained, both with padded headboards. But in the third one there was a four-poster draped in blue satin.

'They must have been millionaires what lived here,' was Willie's passing comment.

'How many rooms are there really, Dad?' Katie had a vivid mental picture of relating the wonder of this house to her friend Sue when she went to her party next week, and not only to Sue, but to that swanky piece Maureen Cuthbert and her cronies.

'Well, there's twelve main ones; that's not counting halls and the utility room, nor the attics. Oh, you must see the attics. There's one full of old bits of furniture. . . .And something could be resurrected from them, I can tell you.'

They oohed and aahed through the attics and over the odd bits of broken furniture. And when Bill pointed out

116

there was a small stream running into the mere but told them that they weren't getting him down there today, Rupert offered to go with them. And Nell, being ever tactful, said to Fiona as she held out the child, 'Here, take her. I want to go and look at that kitchen, and especially that utility room, so I can describe it to Bert.'

'Come and sit down.' Bill led the way back into the dining room; and when Fiona was seated with the child in her arms, he stood looking down at her, saying, 'Well, what d'you think?'

'It's a wonderful place, Bill, but it's really out of our line, isn't it?'

'What d'you mean, out of our line?'

'Well, what I mean is, the cost. Even if you could get it, it would be a burden on our shoulders, on your shoulders.'

'Well let me tell you, Mrs B, that it's already a burden on me shoulders because it is ours. It was signed and sealed on Tuesday.'

'Bill!'

'Sit yourself down again, woman.'

'But . . . but how on earth! And it needs more furnishing and. . . .'

'I know all the "buts" and "ands", I've been through them. And my name's very good at the bank. They would advance me twice as much.'

'Twice as much as what, Bill?' There was an anxious note in her voice.

'Well, now, Mrs B.' – he pulled up a chair and sat opposite to her, his knees touching hers – 'it's been on the market for over a year. Houses are not selling, not like this, not at this price, not around here. Under the hundred thousand, they are, but when you get up to two-hundred thousand plus. . . .*All right*! *All right*! Sit down, woman. Look, you'll drop her if you're not careful.' He put his hand out and laid it on the child. And she said, 'Over two-hundred thousand?'

117

'Yes, it was going for two-hundred and twenty-five thousand, a year ago. And it was worth it. I looked at it then and laughed. It was just before I got the contract and it seemed as far away then as the contract did. But then I was too busy to think much about it until three months ago when I saw it was still on the market and down to two-hundred and ten thousand. And then last month, I understood with a bit of manoeuvring one could get it for two-hundred or a bit less, 'cos the old couple wanted to get away and join their daughter down in the West country; and they didn't want to leave their house empty because of the vandals, and believe me they would have been in in two shakes of a lamb's tail. Anyway, I got them down to a hundred and ninety thousand.'

When Fiona closed her eyes, he said, 'Look dear. That's nothin' the day. You should see what property's going for in Newcastle.'

'This is not Newcastle, Bill. But a hundred and ninety thousand. And the interest!'

'Oh, I didn't have to have a mortgage for all that. You know as well as I do, there's quite a bit in the kitty now.'

'But it's got to be furnished.'

'We can take that in our stride. And we've certainly got lots of bits and pieces back home, haven't we?'

Her face brightened as she said now, 'What would that bring?'

'Oh.' He put his head back, and then, looking at her again, he said, 'I needn't start to reckon up; I've been into all that an' all. You'd get eighty thousand for it the morrow.'

'Never, Bill. And look at the town, most people out of work.'

'It won't attract the people out of work, dear. But there's all these little factories going up and there's what you call the executive group looking for good houses. Now it's a corner house and it's got a good garden back and front. And apart from the one at the top end it's in the best situation in

118

the avenue. And it's in good repair. Oh yes, you'll get eighty.'

'Well, that's something.'

'Aye, that's something.' But there's something I want to put to you. It's your house. It's your money. *Listen. Listen. Listen.*' He was wagging his finger at her now. 'I'm lookin' ahead. This contract is like pennies from heaven but it's not going to last forever, another year or so, or fifteen months, that's if they decide to alter the plans and make that extra row of shops, 'cos as we know there's no more sites like this in these parts. It'll just be smaller jobs, at least here; but I've got a feelin' I can go further afield now. Yet, nothing's ever sure. So you're going into business, Mrs B, in case I go flat.'

'What! What are you talking about?'

'Listen to me, woman. You know Kingsley's garage? Yes, of course you do. Well, you know, it's a scruffy little place, but it wasn't always like that. When Arthur Jones had it, it was a smart affair. He lived above it, and everything was spruce. Then he had to be knocked down by one of his own cars. But since Kingsley took it over . . . well, he's as thick as two planks and he's never engaged a decent mechanic, and so they've lost trade and he's selling, or he's tryin' to, and has been for some time. So he's another who won't quibble about bargainin'. So, I suggest, Mrs B, that you take your eighty thousand and you invest it in the garage business, because, looking ahead, I think we should have our fingers in more than one pie. And people will always be wantin' cars. Many would rather have their own car than their house, or eat. Bloody fools. But there it is, that's life. We could do the place up, put a good man in, a real mechanic, in the flat above. Get some plants and greenery around that front court, and it's a big forecourt. He's got it covered with old run-down bangers now. Well, we won't deal in run-down bangers, not at Bailey's garage . . . Mrs Bailey's garage.'

'Oh, Bill!'

'Don't say oh, Bill! like that. What d'you think really?'

'Well' – she hesitated – 'I think it's a good thing to have. . . .'

'Two strings to your bow.'

'Yes. Yes, two strings to your bow.'

'And perhaps a third, who knows? Anyway, that's settled. Now there's nothin' for you to worry about; all you've got to do is to get this place to your likin', furnished that is, and don't skimp; at the same time don't go mad. Come on.' He drew her up from the chair. 'Let's go and face the mob and find out if Nell has stripped the utility room yet.'

He was making for the door when he turned and said, 'We're lucky, you know, to have her . . . Nell.'

'Oh, I've always felt we're lucky to have Nell, Bill.'

'Aye. Well, I'll take some of that back; she's all right in her place. When I think it's just on two years ago, before you went into hospital and thought you were goin' to peg out, that you had it all planned for me to marry her. Well, she told me plainly that she wouldn't marry me if the rest of the world were dead. And I told her that if she wasn't on earth and was an angel, I still wouldn't look the side she was on, or words to that effect.'

They went out laughing, to meet the avalanche coming in at the front door.

'It's wonderful, Dad.'

'Oh, Mam! there's like a little waterfall at the bottom; it's made up of stones and the water's rippling over it, tumbling and twisting into a little pool.'

'Oh, the poet's on his feet.'

It was noticeable that Willie didn't turn and snarl at Katie, but said, 'Well, clever chops, you said yourself it was bonny.'

And it was noticeable too that Katie didn't threaten to slap his face, but said, 'Yes, it is. It would be lovely in the summer, Mam; you could sit on the rocks and paddle your feet.'

120

'Why would you want to do that when you've got a pool to swim in?'

They looked at Bill in silence for a moment, until Mark said, 'You mean that, Dad?'

'Aye, that's what I mean, Mark. I mean that this is your home from now on.'

Mark, Willie, Katie, and Mamie, were all clinging round him now, popping and crying out their excitement, while Fiona and Nell stood at one side looking at them; and standing apart were Rupert and Sammy. And Rupert, looking down at Sammy, said in a false whisper, 'We'll have to keep our noses clean, Sammy, and try to get an invite to this place.'

For answer Sammy said, 'Don't matter.'

And this caused a bark from Bill that drowned the others' voices: 'What d'you mean, it don't matter?' he demanded.

'Well, too far out; not like your other house.'

'There's a bus, isn't there? And you can get a bike.'

'Don't want a bike. Me da's gona get a car, a new one.'

'Good for him. Then you can come in your da's car, can't you?'

'Might.'

'No might about it, Sammy Love. Anyway, you'll be here more than you'll be at home, if I know anything.'

'If me da goes along the line I'll have to go to me granny's. Jinny'll not stay.'

Bill pushed the children aside, then went and stood over the minute figure, bawling at him now, 'Trust you to put a spanner in the works! Everybody laughin' and happy 'cos they've got this grand house an' you puttin' the damper on things. What's up with you? And you.' He looked at Rupert, 'What's up with you an' all?'

'Well, I'm out in the cold too, Mr Bailey. This house is out of my way; I don't see how I'm going to visit so often.'

There was a cry from Katie and she was clinging on to

121

Rupert's arm now, shouting, 'You can come and live here. You can have the granny flat. I'll cook for you.'

'Oh my God! Then we can expect a funeral.'

Of a sudden all their attention was turned towards Nell, who added, 'Does anybody realise that the gas, water, and electricity have been cut off in this house? Not that it matters because we haven't any tea, sugar, milk, or crockery. And what I'm needing at this moment is a strong cup of tea. Now do you think, Mr Bailey, that you can get us home as quickly as you got us here?'

'You know what I'd like to do with you,' said Bill, now pushing the tribe out of the door; 'I'd like to slap your face for you, both sides.'

'Bigger men than you have had that desire, Mr Bailey, bigger men than you.'

So amid laughter, they piled into the cars and drove away from the house that was to be their new home.

7

The magistrate was addressing the man in the dock. 'You, Mr Love,' he was saying slowly, 'have acquired the habit over the years of acting first and thinking later. Were we all to hit out when we heard someone speak derisively of us then I for one would have been behind bars years ago.'

A titter went round the court at this. Mr Arthur Fellmore was known for his witty quips. The clerks and solicitors waited for them, and in this case they hadn't as yet been disappointed. It was whether he or the Irishman would come out on top, but of course he had the upper hand, and the Irishman was well aware of it. Yet that didn't stop him from saying, 'Then you've had a taste of it, yer Worship, but bein' more sensible than meself you kept yer hands down an'. . . .'

'Mister Love!' The magistrate's voice expressed patience. 'I do not wish to know your opinion of my mental restraint; but I want you to understand that your actions are not to be tolerated. You were, I am told, in charge of a gang of workers and when the plaintiff was about to carry out an order that you had given him but had the effrontery to express his opinion of you, what did you do?'

'I did what any man in me place would have done, yer Worship, I closed his mouth for him.'

The hammer hitting the desk subdued the laughter.

'I'll thank you, Mr Love, to listen to what I am saying and not interrupt. Do you understand me?'

'I do yer Worship, and I'm sorry. It's me tongue.'

It was observed that the magistrate lowered his head and closed his eyes for a moment before going on: 'You did not only close the defendant's mouth but you broke his nose and put him in hospital for a week.'

When someone pushed a paper slowly along the table and under the magistrate's nose, he corrected himself: 'Oh, barely two days. Well, that was enough. But since that time I understand the defendant has been unable to work and has been suffering from shock.'

'Pardon me for sayin' so, yer Worship, but he's always shocked by work, even the word shocks him.'

'*Silence in court!*'

'I have warned you, Mr Love.'

'Aye, yer Worship. But God in heaven! it's more than a man can stand to hear him made out as a poor sick individual when we all know he's. . . .'

'*Mr Love!*'

Davey dropped his head, and there followed a heavy silence in the court room. When he again looked up it was to meet a warning glance from Bill sitting at the back of the court; in fact, Bill was rubbing his hand through his hair in an agitated fashion.

'You are a man, Mr Love, I'm afraid, who'll never learn, either to keep his mouth shut or to keep his hands to himself. Now I am going to pass sentence on you, but before doing so I may tell you the bench is taking into consideration that when you used your hands once before, you were the means of bringing to justice two potential murderers who are now serving sentences for their crime. So this fact alone causes us to temper the punishment we might have given to you for your latest episode. Therefore, we will use leniency and commit you to one hundred hours of community work.

Also you will pay a fine of one hundred pounds. And I may add, Mr Love, that if you are wise you will decide never to appear in this court again, at least when I'm on the bench. You understand?'

'I do, yer Worship, I do. And honest to God! I promise you you've seen the last of me and me of you. Thank you. Thank you, yer Worship.'

The court stood; the magistrates departed.

Bill and his solicitor went up to Davey and the solicitor said, 'Well, not too bad, eh?'

Davey, who was visibly sweating now, took out a handkerchief and rubbed it round his mouth before saying, 'I think it was pretty stiff.'

Bill too now nodding at the solicitor: 'A hundred working hours and a hundred quid. Phew! Yes, I think I agree with Davey.'

'You don't know our dear Mr Fellmore,' said the solicitor under his breath. 'He must have had a good weekend. I wouldn't have been surprised if he had got the bench to send you down for at least three months.' He was nodding at Davey. 'I can tell you you've got to thank, not only your friend here' – he inclined his head towards Bill – 'but one or two friends in the force. They raked out the facts that Potter had been in trouble up in London, nothing very big, all petty; and his Worship must have had this made known to him. And, of course, Potter did throw those planks at you before you went for him.'

'Oh, yes, yes.' Bill nodded his agreement.

'What'll I have to do in that hundred hours?'

'Oh, all kinds of things. You had better come along with me now to the office. One thing I can tell you, you won't have many week-ends free, or even nights, until you've served your sentence.' The solicitor laughed now as he added, 'You can stop sweating, it's over. But as his Worship said, I'd watch those hands of yours in the future.'

Following on this remark Davey was put to the test sooner

than he could have expected: he was passing by a group of people in the hallway when a voice said, 'Community service! He should have been sent along the bloody line, the big-mouthed galoot.'

'Now! now! now!' said another voice.

Bill actually felt Davey's body jerk, but he noticed that he looked straight ahead, his eyes very wide, his chin thrust out; the solicitor had noted Davey's reaction and he was quick to remark on it: 'You should have ten out of ten for first test passed,' he said.

Davey made no remark on this, nor did Bill, for both of them knew how near to another court case Davey had been just a moment previously.

Davey was warmed and touched by the greeting he received when he returned with Bill to the house. Except for Mark, who was at school, all the children were at home.

'They didn't want you as governor at Durham then?' was Nell's greeting when he entered the sitting-room.

'No, Nell; no. They don't know what they're missin', do they? Now I ask you.'

Fiona said, 'Oh, thank goodness it's over. And you won't mind doing community work, will you?'

'Mrs B. I'd walk on me hands on hot cinders, anything rather than take that van to Durham.'

Katie said, 'If they had sent you I would have come and visited you. I would. I really would.'

'Thank you, Katie, me love; and I'd have been delighted to see you. There wouldn't have been a prettier visitor in that prison.'

What Willie said was, 'I told him. I told him all along' – he nodded at Sammy – 'I told him that they wouldn't dare send you to prison, 'cos you'd knock the he . . .' – he choked on the word and it brought spluttering laughter from Katie, Mamie, and also Nell, but a look of reprimand from his mother, and so he finished with, 'Well, what I

126

mean is, he would have seen them off. Wouldn't you, Mr Love?'

'Well, I would have done me best, lad. I would have done me best. An' what's me son got to say to me? He hasn't opened his mouth.' Davey looked around him as if appealing to the others, saying, 'Not a word. Not a word.'

All eyes were on Sammy waiting for an answer; but for once there was no response, only a thrusting out of the lips and a knobbling of the small chin.

Bill broke the embarrassed silence by handing a glass to Davey, saying, 'Get that down you, and then get home and out of those fancy togs and back on the job. And, as Nell says, they'll have the flag out for you.'

'Oh aye? I can see them, and hear 'em: they'll scoff me lugs off. But what odds.'

'If they scoff your lugs off it'll be in a kindly fashion. Should it happen though that one or another should say somethin' that isn't to your likin', Mr Love, just you remember what his Worship said.'

'You have no need to press that home, boss, no need whatever. Anyway, thanks for the drink. Thanks for everything.' He stood up and looked around him. 'And I'll say this: there's one thing I'm sure of in this world, 'tis I'll never have much money but I feel rich – at this minute I feel like a millionaire, 'cos I've got friends like you, large and small, friends like you.' On this he turned to make for the door; and when Sammy scampered after him, Willie followed, demanding, 'Where are you going?'

'I'm goin' home with me da.'

'But he's going to work.'

'I know that; I've got ears.'

'Will you come back after?'

'Aye. Aye. I'll come back after. But now *I'm goin' home.*'

'All right, all right, don't bawl. How long will you be?'

'As long as it takes.'

Davey had paused to wait for his son and now said to

127

him, 'Come on you, an' shut that trap. 'Tis a pity you take after me, 'tis that.'

The family had followed them into the hall and so Nell, who had opened the door, did not immediately close it after Davey and Sammy, for they all stood watching the very tall man and the very small boy walking down the drive together.

When Bill said, 'What am I thinkin' about? I could have given them a lift,' Fiona put in quietly, 'They'll have more time to be together on their own when they're walking.'

'There's the phone!' Nell said, and Bill turned quickly away towards the stairs, saying, 'If it's for me, tell them I'll be there in the next ten minutes.'

After picking up the phone Nell listened for a moment, then, lifting her hand, she flapped her fingers slowly towards Fiona. And Fiona, taking the phone from her, said, 'Hello.'

'Fiona.'

'Yes, Mother?'

'What's this I'm hearing?'

'What are you hearing now, Mother?'

'I've heard you're moving.'

'Yes; that's right.'

'And of course, I'm the last to know. I just couldn't believe it. When was all this settled?'

'Just before Christmas, Mother.'

'And today is the eighth of January, and you've known all the time.'

'Mother!' Fiona's voice lost all its evenness and she was almost yelling now: 'You went away on Christmas Eve to stay with friends, didn't you? You didn't tell me what time you were coming back, or if you were coming back. What is more, we weren't on very amicable terms, so you wouldn't expect me to run and tell you what was happening here. Anyway, you made your opinion very plain when we last met. So, yes, we are moving, and soon.'

There was a pause before Mrs Vidler's voice came again, saying now, 'And where, may I ask, are you moving to?'

128

'Well, Mother, for your information, I can tell you that it would be regarded as a small private estate. It is called, Burnstead Mere House.'

'*Burnstead Mere?* You can't mean? You don't mean the Olivers' place? Sir . . . Sir Roger Oliver's house beyond Durham?'

'Yes, that is the house.'

'But . . . but it is a large place. It's a. . . .'

'I know, Mother, it's a large place, with its own swimming pool and large grounds.'

'You're flying high, aren't you?'

'Not as high as my husband eventually hopes to fly, Mother.'

'Oh, come off it. Don't take that attitude with me. You can't make a silk purse out of a sow's ear, and I've told you that before.'

Fiona drew her head back from the phone. She turned and looked to where Nell was standing near the kitchen door and she actually lifted her clenched fist and shook it. Then her mother's voice came again: 'And what about me?'

'What about you, Mother?'

'What if I need help and you are miles away? You forget I'm a woman on my own.'

'What I don't forget, Mother, is that you are surrounded by your so-called friends. You are rarely in the house; and what is more you are no longer an elderly lady, are you, kicking sixty? You are now, so you would have one understand, a woman in her forties. You could marry again someone of your own age, whichever one you choose.'

'You're being bitchy, aren't you?'

'Yes, Mother, it's my turn, and not before time.'

'Well, I can be bitchy too, dear, and I'll say this: the reason he is putting you in a big house out in the wilds is to hide the monstrosity he's presented you with.'

When Fiona dropped the phone onto the stand and placed her hands on the edge of the narrow table and, bending

129

forward, rested her head against the wall, Nell came to her immediately and put her arm around her shoulder. 'What is it?' she said. 'But need I ask? Oh, she's a devil of a woman that! Come on. Come on. Come and sit down.'

Nell now led her into the sitting-room, saying hastily, 'Don't cry. For goodness sake don't cry; he'll be down in a minute. And if she said . . . oh, I know, it isn't an "if", she said something about the child. Well, you know what that'll do to him. Come on. Come on. Pull yourself together. Look, I'll get a drink.' She quickly poured out a sherry.

'Get that down you,' she said, handing it to Fiona. 'Oh, here he comes.'

Fiona turned and looked towards Bill, but she didn't rise from the couch.

'You all right?'

'Yes, yes.'

'Who was that on the phone?'

When she hesitated and looked towards Nell, he said, 'Oh, you needn't tell me. What had she to say this time?'

Fiona forced herself to smile. 'I told her about the house, and she wanted to know what I was going to do about her, this poor old lady left on her own.'

'Oh, tell her we've got a granny flat; tell her not to worry.' Then bending over her, he said, 'Mrs Bailey, I'd burn that house down before I'd let her into it. So never let your daughterly compassion get the better of you. You understand?'

'Yes, Mr Bailey, I understand.'

He bent and kissed her; then looking at Nell, he said, 'See that she has a rest; there's plenty time for the packing.'

'Yes, master. Will do, master.'

'And the same to you.' He went out laughing.

Taking her seat beside Fiona, Nell said, 'What did she say to knock you out like that?'

'Well, Nell, she said the only thing he was taking the house for was to hide the monstrosity he had given me.'

'Oh, my God! She didn't!'

'Yes, she did. And you know something? That's what a lot of people will think. Oh yes, they will. Oh yes, they will. It's the way of the world, and you can't escape it.'

PART TWO

THE FIRST BIRTHDAY

1

'Come on, Angela.'

'Come on. Come on, Angie, crawl.'

'Come on, pet. Come on.'

Bill, Katie, and Willie, were kneeling at the end of an imitation white fur rug that flanked the large open stone fireplace in which a log fire was blazing. Mark, Sammy, and Mamie knelt to the side of it and all their attention was on the child who lay on its stomach with its elbows half hidden in the pile as it rocked from side to side.

'She's trying. She'll do it! Come on, my angel, come on.' Bill held out his hands towards her, and the child, its head up, smiled widely at him, making a gurgling sound. And at this Sammy said, 'She won't do it till she's ready.'

Fiona, who was sitting on the couch with Nell and Bert, nodded towards Sammy: 'You're right, Sammy,' she said; 'she won't do it till she's ready. I'm told I didn't walk until I was nearly two.'

'She'll walk before she's two. Come on, pet. Come on.'

Fiona looked down on Bill where he was sitting back on his haunches clapping his hands. How that man loved that child. She loved her too, but not with his intensity. She doubted that had the child been other than she was he

135

would have showered the love on her that he did. He never came into the house but he made straight for her; and whenever he could he held her, bouncing her in his arms, or holding her high above his head, always taking a delight, it would seem, in her gurgling at him. She was a happy child, she rarely cried. However, she understood from the doctor – a new one since they had come to live here – that, as for walking and talking, she would likely be a late developer. He was a very nice man, this Doctor Pringle. He was one of a small group of three doctors and he had told her that there were eight such children in their practice. And he had added, they were all happy and lovable. He was very reassuring, and there were times, she had to admit to herself, she needed reassurance. That was one thing she couldn't get from Bill, because he didn't need it; well, if he did, he hid it, and hid it well.

But how different everything had been since they had come into this beautiful house. Sometimes she didn't know whether it was the house or the child; but no, she had to give credit to the child because the children had behaved themselves from the day she had brought Angela home, that awful day when she had been laden down with guilt and shame. And if she was true to herself she must admit that there remained a little of both in her; and she longed to erase it all from her, especially the shame, for why should she be ashamed of this child who had been the means of making her family into a complete unit again? She had been not only irritated but worried by the feeling that had been showing itself between Katie and Willie. Not only did they lash out with their tongues but with their fists. Then their spoiling of Mamie had made her become quite cheeky at times. Mark was the only one who had remained himself. Yet he went for both Katie and Willie, and, of course, they retaliated likewise. But now all that was as if it had never been: she was often amazed to see how Katie and Willie would give way to each other in nursing the child.

136

'Look!' cried Willie now; 'she's moved her back leg. She's bringing it up.'

'She hasn't got a back leg, you idiot!' Katie pushed him.

'But yes: she is! She is, Dad. Look! She is.'

'She is that,' said Bill in awestruck tones as if he was experiencing a minor miracle. 'See that! Mrs B?'

'What I see,' said Fiona, 'is that she is being roasted by that fire. Give her here!' She pushed Mark on the shoulder, and he, bending forward, lifted up the child; then, swinging round on his knees, he put her onto Fiona's lap.

'A burglar could walk into this place and clear half the house and nobody would notice.'

The children sprang up and all eyes were turned towards the door at the end of the long room. And it was Katie who ran forward, saying, 'You're back then. You're back.'

As she linked her arm in Rupert's he said, 'Well, if I'm not, my ghost couldn't keep away.'

'Hello there.' Bill walked forward to greet Rupert, saying to Katie, 'Stop being a nuisance, you. Let the fella get in.'

'Katie!' Fiona too called to her daughter now, quietly but firmly; then she added, 'Take Rupert's coat.'

'When did you get back from Scotland? Sit yourself down. Do you want a drink?'

'I got back last night. And yes, oh yes, I could do with a drink.'

'Tea or coffee?' It was Katie by his side again; and he smiled at her and said, 'May I have something a little stronger, miss?'

Katie looked towards Bill. He nodded, then turned back to Rupert and said, 'Would you like it hot? You look frozen. A lot of snow up there?'

Again Rupert answered two questions at once: 'That would be very acceptable; hot; and brown sugar.' He smacked his lips. 'And yes, there was quite a covering of snow. Three-foot drifts in parts. You'll get it next.'

'How is Lady Kingdom?'

137

Rupert turned to Fiona and answered her: 'Rather lost. They had been married over fifty years, you know; and they'd known each other ten years before that. But her family are very supportive: they all want her to go and live with them, but, as she said, she would then have one leg in Somerset, the other in Jersey, and an arm in Harrogate.'

'What's going to happen to the Manor?' It was Nell asking the question, and he said, 'Oh, naturally, that's got to be sold, Nell. She'd never go back there. Anyway, the upkeep is phenomenal, and it wants so much doing to it. They'll likely pull it down and sell the land.'

'Will they now?' Bill's head was nodding, and Rupert replied, 'Yes, they will now, Bill. And I was thinking that you should look into it.'

'I certainly shall, Rupert, I certainly shall, because the boundary of the estate is cheek by jowl with the last row we're on now. Yes, Rupert, I certainly shall look into it. Anyway, come on into the kitchen and I'll make your toddy.'

As Rupert rose, so, too, did Katie, only to be checked by Fiona, saying, 'Katie, stay where you are.'

'Oh! Mam.'

'Never mind, oh! Mam.'

'Could you do with a hot 'un, Bert? No; I'm not enticing you to break the pledge, man, but hot ginger ale isn't bad with lemon. I've had it meself. Good for a cold.'

'Thanks all the same, Bill, but I don't trust you.'

'My God! What d'you think of that?' He turned to Rupert. 'He's tellin' me I'd put a dollop of the hard stuff in.'

'Well, that wouldn't surprise me either, Bill.'

Bill led the way from the room, saying, 'I read somewhere that some bloke said if you could count on one hand two real friends you were lucky. He didn't know what he was talking about.'

When the door closed on them, Bert rose from the couch, saying to the boys, 'What about a game of table tennis? Sammy and me will take you two on.' He nodded from

138

Mark to Willie, and Willie cried, 'Fine! Fine!' Then turning to Fiona, he asked her, 'What time's the birthday tea, Mam?'

Fiona glanced at Nell, who just shrugged her shoulders as she said, 'Half-past four, say. You've got a good hour.'

As the boys went to scamper from the room, Bert said to Katie, 'You coming along?'

'No. What would I do? Just stand and watch.'

'We could take turns.'

'No thanks, Bert; I'm all right here. I'm going to read.'

'OK. Everyone to their fancy.'

Nell was the next to rise from the couch, saying to Fiona, 'Well, I'll go and put the final touches and set another place for Rupert, that's if he'll be staying.'

'Oh yes, he will, 'cos he's got no place else to go.'

Both Fiona and Nell turned to look at Katie, who then said, 'Well, he hasn't, has he? I mean now that the Manor is going to be sold.'

Nell again shrugged her shoulers and went out. And Fiona said to her daughter who was curled up in the corner of the couch, 'Come here, Katie.'

Slowly Katie unwound her legs before hitching herself up towards her mother, who was now leaning forward and placing the child on a cushion in the middle of a large armchair to the side of the couch; and having settled the child she turned to her daughter, and, taking both her hands, said, 'My dear, I must talk to you about Rupert. Please! Please, don't pull your hands away; and don't look like that, dear. You have been such a good daughter to me this past year; we've never had a cross word and I don't want us to have one now. But . . . but it's for your own good I'm going to say, you must stop' – she was going to use the words pestering; instead she softened it with, 'paying so much attention to Rupert.'

'Oh! Mam. Mam.' The words were a cross between a cry and a protest.

'I know, I know how you feel. I felt like that once, just

the same as you do now. He happened to be a greengrocer and I couldn't wait for his weekly visit. Don't . . . please don't pull away from me. Rupert is a man; he is thirty years old. He is admittedly very attractive. And you are a twelve-year-old girl.'

'I'm nearly thirteen and older men marry young girls. The film star Frank. . . .'

'What film stars do and ordinary people do are vastly different things.'

'Do you consider you and Dad ordinary, Mam?'

This was a poser, but Fiona had to say, 'Yes, yes, I do.'

'Well, you are only thirty-two and Dad is forty-nine; so what are you talking about? There are seventeen years between you, and . . . and I could be married when I'm sixteen.'

'*Katie*! *Katie*! What are you saying? And what are you thinking? Oh, I know what you're thinking. Well, let me tell you that Rupert will never marry anyone. Never!'

'What . . . what are you saying? He's already married?'

'No; he's not already married. More's the pity.'

'Then, why can't he marry?'

'There is a reason.'

'I . . . I don't believe you, Mam. You are just saying this to put me off. But it won't; I'll wait. I know how I feel. I'll wait.'

'*Katie*!' She now pulled her hands from Katie's and clapped one across her mouth, realising that she had shouted.

And she expected Katie to turn now and fly from the room, but the girl just sat, staring at her, her lips trembling, her eyes wet with unshed tears.

'You're being cruel, Mam. I . . . I love Rupert.'

'Katie' – Fiona closed her eyes and brought her chin tight into her neck – 'girls of your age all go through this pash experience. . . .'

'It isn't a pash. Nancy Burke's got a pash on Mr Richards

and Mary Parkin has a pash on Miss Taylor, and so have other girls. But I haven't got a pash on Rupert. It isn't like that. I know it isn't. *I know it isn't.*'

Looking at her daughter, Fiona thought: very likely it isn't; these things happen. And she is a sensible girl. She's always been sensible, always older than her years. She . . . she must tell her.

She turned and put her hand out and straightened the dribble bib on the baby's pretty frilly dress; then she turned back to Katie and said, 'Do you think you're old enough to keep a secret?'

Katie did not reply, and so she went on, 'If I tell you why Rupert will never marry, will you promise not to divulge it or let him know you know the reason?'

When again she got no answer from her daughter, only that wide bright-eyed moist stare, she said, 'Rupert was to be married to his childhood sweetheart. Everything was arranged. The young girl was a distant relative of Sir Charles and Lady Kingdom. One night just before the wedding, they attended a dance. He had gone to get the car to take her home. When he returns she's not there. She was found the next morning in the shrubbery. She had been –' she hesitated, then went on, 'she had been raped and hit over the head with some instrument. And this resulted in her being in a coma for a long time, and from then has never spoken. But she has dreadful screaming fits, and is now in Hetherington Hospital, where she will likely remain until she dies. And she's still a young girl, frozen into the time when that dreadful thing happened. That's why Rupert acted as secretary to Sir Charles, in order to stay near her. And that is why, since Sir Chalres has died, he will now remain here in order to be near her, for as he told your father, he feels he is married to her, that she is his wife in everything but name.'

Her daughter's face was now drained of colour; the eyes were wide; the moisture had gone from them, and in its

141

place was a look of what she could only describe as hopeless-ness. But then Katie's next words contradicted her assump-tion, for she said, 'She could die sometime.'

'Oh! Katie, how can you say such a thing. Anyway, she could live for years, years, and years. And let me tell you that Rupert lives in hope of her recovering, no matter what the doctor says, because a while ago she called his name, and that was the first time she had spoken. So get it out of your head, girl' – her voice was harsh now – 'Rupert is not for you; nor does he want you. He thinks of you as a child. He puts up with your fussing, let me tell you, because he's a gentleman and it would be bad manners to thrust you off.'

She watched the colour flood back into her daughter's face, saw the lips tremble and the tears spurt from her eyes. And when her arms went out and pulled her into her embrace Katie muttered, 'Oh, Mam. Mam,' and she mur-mured, 'There, there.'

'Oh, Mam, I'm so unhappy, I . . . I want to die.'

'I know, dear, I know; but that feeling will pass.'

'No; it never will. It never will.'

'I promise you it will. It won't be long before you find another boy; in fact, I know someone who already has his eye on you. In the words of a story, I would say he is enamoured of you. Mark laughs because Roland is always talking about you.'

'Oh; Roland Featherstone. He's only a boy!'

'He is fast growing out of being a boy: he's turned fourteen, nearly fifteen and very attractive.'

'Oh! Mam, be quiet! Be quiet! I . . . I can't help it about Rupert and . . . and that woman.'

'Girl, Katie.'

'Well, whoever, I . . . I'll go on loving him.'

'That's up to you, my dear, if you want to cause yourself pain. But you've got to also tell yourself that he will never love you other than as a nice girl. Now look, dry your eyes, the others will be coming back shortly. Better still, go out

142

of the side door, through the conservatory and up the back way to your room. Wash your face and put some cream on. You made up very well the other night for the school party, a bit too heavy in parts, especially round the eyes. Really you don't need mascara; your lashes are dark and long and they enhance your eyes. I'd always go lightly with make-up around the eyes if I were you. Go on now. Wait a moment!' She grabbed her arm. 'You won't let Rupert know what I've told you.'

'No. No, Mam.'

'Go on now, dear.' . . .

Meanwhile in the kitchen Rupert was saying to Bill, 'But I know nothing whatever about cars except how to drive them.'

'You're not expected to know anything about cars, man. Mechanics can see to that side of the busines. But it needs somebody there with a presence like yours, a fella who can talk to customers and give an air of class to the place. Oh, aye, I know, I'm rubbin' it on thick; but you must have the same opinion of yourself if you spoke the truth. Anyway, Fuller and his wife are goin' next week. I took him on the references and they were glowing. He must have written them out himself. Aye, there was one thing he could write all right, his expense accounts. My God! If you saw how much it cost me for him to even run into Newcastle. But when he went to Harrogate and took his wife and two kids with him and stayed in a five-star hotel, well, that put the finish to Mr Fuller. Anyway, there it is. There's a flat above, and it's a very pleasant flat. The back looks onto fields, the only farm left in this district I should think. What is more, I want somebody who can give orders in a nice way, an' you're used to that, for you've been the mouthpiece of the old boy for years. . . .Oh I know. An' so did Lady Kingdom. She said as much to me: "What would we do without Rupert to soothe the savage breasts that a certain gentleman creates." She was meaning Sir Charles. And I don't know what screw the old fella gave you, but I'll meet it and a little more likely. You'll also get your cut on sales. As for the fellas there: two are good mechanics, but the third one's goin'. He's simply a greaser and I'm not payin' a greaser mechanic's wages, I can tell you that. And as yet there's only one young fella in the showroom. He'll come on, I'm sure. He had to do the business when Fuller went on his jaunts. From what I understand his wife liked jaunts: hardly a day but they didn't take a jaunt. There'll have to be a lot of reorganising done; I'll leave that to you. You've been in enough garages, I'm sure, to see the ones you'd go back to and the ones you wouldn't. With the right management and the right work-men that place could be a little gold mine. What about it?'

'I'm very grateful, Bill. As you know I can't leave the county. But only this morning I rented a flat for three months.'

'Aw, don't worry about that; we'll make that good. Here, shake hands on it.'

As they shook hands Rupert said, 'Thank you, Bill. You've been a good friend to me.'

'I wasn't at first; now, was I?'

'No; no, you certainly weren't: you played the jealous husband to a T.'

'Yes, I did; and that would have gone on, mind, if you hadn't told me the situation. And I shouldn't have been a bit surprised if I'd done a Davey Love on you.'

'By the way, how is Davey these days?'

'Oh, the same as ever. If that fella was being hanged you'd have to laugh at him. You know, he made more friends when he was doing his community sentence than half a dozen men would make in their life-times. You'll see him later; he's comin' to the tea, so we'll get a laugh if nothin' else. He'll likely shock Miss Isherwood; but then, I don't know.'

'Have I met her?'

'Oh no; I forgot. She's come on the scene since you've

been away. Our scene, I should have said, for she's been on the scene for longer than this house has stood. She lives in the bungalow just down the road. It's the only other habitation around here. Fiona met up with her when she was out with the pram one day and they got on talkin'. Our land here belonged to her grandfather. The bungalow has been extended from an old stone cottage which was their original home, so she tells us. Yes, her grandfather owned all this land. Of course, it was merely fields then, and he sold it to Mr Oliver, that was before he was knighted. He built this place, and I am glad he did because where would you find a more lovely house, Rupert, eh? – and a happier family – because somethin' seems to have happened to everybody since we came here.'

Bill paused and looked away for a moment before he added, 'But I don't think that's quite true; I think we might have something to thank the child for. She has linked the lot of us in a chain around her, a happy chain. Anyway,' – his voice rose again – 'Miss Caroline Isherwood is comin' to Angela's first birthday party. She is a librarian by the way.'

'Librarian? Oh. Young, middle-aged, or getting on a bit?'

'Young, my dear sir, young. I don't know her age, but I would say it would be twenty-four, twenty-five; not good looking, no interestin' face, but very smart. You know, a figure like two laths.' He pushed Rupert on the shoulder. 'Davey's lost his lady-love, the barmaid, you know. I think it was all to do with Sammy. Sammy didn't take to her. I wonder if he'll take to the librarian? That would be funny, wouldn't it?'

'It would be funnier if the librarian took to Davey.'

'Aye; you've said something there, it certainly would. But still, you never know, stranger things happen. Have you finished that toddy?'

'Yes; and it's gone down to my toes.'

'Well, let's get back and see if we've been missed. Oh –'

he nodded at Rupert now – 'you'll have been missed all right, Katie's taken you over. But I'm tellin' you, she's a determined young miss, that; you'll have to slap her down if she gets a bit too possessive like. You know what I mean. Young lasses like that want slappin' down. So you slap her down. You have my permission.'

'Oh, Bill! I could never slap Katie down. Anyway, she's just a child.'

He was about to repudiate this and say, 'Katie's no child, lad. Katie's no child,' but then if Rupert thought that Katie was just a child, well and good.

PART THREE

THE SECOND BIRTHDAY

1

$\blacklozenge$

Bill pulled his car to an abrupt stop on the wide forecourt of the garage, jumped out and almost ran into the showroom, then wended his way through a number of new cars to the office where Rupert, having seen his approach, had risen from his seat behind his desk. And as Bill came in the door he said, 'I can see by your face it's good news.'

'Aye, lad; I've clinched it.'

'The lot?'

'Aye, the lot. But of course, there's conditions. I knew there would be. All that matters though is we're all set for another spell. By! lad, it's been hard work.'

'Will I get you a cup of tea?'

'No, no; I want more than a cup of tea, man. I'm on me way home, but I thought I'd pop in and tell you because I've got you to thank for this.'

'I've done nothing.'

'You put me onto it and tipped me off as to who to see an' who to deal with. And there's been some sticky individuals.'

'You can take the house down?'

'No, I can't. But that might prove better in the end. It's

149

got to stand in three acres; but I can turn it into some high-class flats.'

'Yes. Yes, that's an idea.'

'Of course that's another thing that'll have to be worked out. But as it stands it's detached houses with not less than a quarter of an acre. They were adamant on that. And that suits me. McGilroy's got good ideas in that head of his. We'll put up some spankers. Aw! lad.' He now pushed Rupert with his doubled fist. 'It's been a long haul and I hadn't Sir Charles's voice for me at the table this time.'

'And he was always for you. He thought a great deal of you, you know, Bill. He used to say, given the chance earlier on and you could have been a captain of industry. But you could still, you know.'

'Huh!' Bill laughed. 'Captain of industry. I'm damn lucky to be second mate, even one of the crew. But no! never one of the crew, not me! But I must get back and tell Fiona. By the way, we'll hold the tea for you.'

'No; don't do that. You know, I won't be able to get there till about seven.'

'Let Mickey close up for you and Joe see to the shop below.'

'I'd rather you didn't wait; I'll pop along later. And you know, I can't think it's a year since her last birthday.'

'Nor me. Her birthday, as you know, was really on Monday; but Nell was under the weather, had been for a couple of days, so we put it off.'

They walked down the showroom together; then as they reached the door it was pushed open and Bill said in some surprise, 'Well! Fancy meetin' you here. What you after? Goin' to buy a car? Oh I can sell you a nice one; it's goin' cheap at the price. Seven thousand, five hundred. I'll knock a hundred off to you. What d'you say?'

Caroline Isherwood smiled widely at Bill and immediately took up his attitude. 'I'm not interested in anything in that range, Mr Bailey,' she said. 'You had a Volvo in last week,

150

in the window there.' She waved her hand airily. 'It was only thirteen thousand. Have you anything in that range still.'

After they had all laughed together, Rupert said, 'She's all ready and waiting. Hang on a minute, and I'll come round the back.' But he seemed hesitant to move. Looking at the smart young woman, Bill said, 'Why don't you pop in more often and see my wife? You'd be very welcome. We hardly catch a glimpse of you and yet you're only down the road.'

'I'm a working girl, Mr Bailey.'

'Aye, I understand that. But there's long evenings and weekends, and you've just said you're on your own. I've thought about you once or twice. Anyway, we're havin' a little birthday party for my daughter. How about it the night?'

Did Bill's sharp eye detect a movement of the head towards Rupert, still standing hesitant. And when she said, 'I have tickets for a concert in Durham,' he said, 'Oh, well; I can't stand up against the concert, I can only put on a turn by a pair called Love, father and son. And I'll bet you won't get as many laughs at your concert as you would from these two.'

'I don't suppose we'll get any laughs from this concert; it's a Mozart.'

'Oh.' Bill pulled a long face. 'Mozart. That fella.' Then his eyes twinkling, he looked at Rupert and said, 'He plays a ukelele, doesn't he?'

'Go on with you!'

He went out, got into the car, started up the engine, then looked through the side window to where, under the bright overhead lights they were both standing shoulder to shoulder. And as he put his foot on the accelerator he said to himself, 'Aye, aye! How long has that been goin' on?' Then he didn't ask why his mind should jump immediately to Katie: she doted on that fella, although she had stopped pawing him about since her mother had that talk with her last year and put her in the picture. Fiona said she'd just had to, and he agreed with her. Katie was thirteen now, nearing fourteen. It was a tricky age with lasses, as it was with lads. And Katie's brain was away beyond her years in all ways. If her marks came below ninety at school she had a crying match. She couldn't bear to be beaten. Well, life would likely knock that out of her but it would take time. She had those teenage years to go through. With one thing and another Fiona had her hands full. Oh yes; for there was Willie too. He wouldn't let himself breathe unless Sammy was about. Then Mamie. My! there was a little madam. She got the surprise of her life last week that one, when he scudded her backside for her. That had given her something to have a tantrum about. All because she couldn't have a gold charm bangle. 'I'll send to my grandfather,' she had said; 'he'll let me have some of my money.' Ooh! by, she thought a cuddy had kicked her. And when she was told that arrangements could be made right away for her to go to Wales and stay with her grandparents she howled. And then there was Mark. But there was no girl trouble with Mark. In a way he could wish there was because he spent too much time round his mother. Yet, he mustn't grumble about that; the boy had been protective of her before he himself had come on the scene. He must remember that. And Mark was a good lad. And what was more these days and while his mind was on them he must remember too that they were all of one accord when it came to the child. But who could help loving her; she gave out love with every breath. And now she was walking and saying a word here and there. And only he himself knew what that meant; even Fiona, as perceptive as she was, didn't realise the effect that child had on him and the feeling she wrought in him. He doubted very much now that, if she had been wholly normal, she would have touched his depth in the way that with her handicap she did.

He went into the house, demanding loudly as he usually did when no one was in sight: 'Where's everybody?'

By the time he had taken off his coat, hat and muffler Fiona had appeared at the top of the broad staircase, calling, 'We're up here, dear.'

She waited until he reached the landing before asking, 'Well, how did it go?'

'It's clinched, lass.'

'Really?'

'Yes. Yes, really.' And putting his hands on her shoulders he bent forward and kissed her on the lips; then looking into her eyes, he said, 'Nothin's goin' to hold that fella back now. The estate contract was big, but this one'll set me name up. These houses will be known as William Bailey's houses. You'll want for nothing: anything you set your heart on in the future you'll have.'

'I've all I want, Bill, and more. I've told you dozens of times. This house is to be our home until they all grow up and, as I've said, even after they've gone, and –' She now poked him in the chest with her finger while she added, 'and when I'm pushing you round in a wheelchair.'

As they walked along the landing he said, 'I called at the garage to tell Rupert because, you know, he went a long way in coaching me as to the temperament of Sir Charles's trustees. And who d'you think called in for her car?'

'Well who? I'm no good at guessing.'

'Our neighbour, Miss Caroline Isherwood.'

'Well, I suppose. . . .Was her car in?'

'Yes; I understand her car's been in for some repair or other; but I seem to detect a closer association than manager and client between them.'

'How do you make that out?'

'Oh, one of my forty senses. And he won't be in to the tea the night. He had previously made an excuse that he couldn't be here before seven. I'd even said we could put the meal back. But no, no. And then Miss Isherwood refused

153

my invitation too. She was goin' to a Mozart concert. Now, I ask you, Mrs B, who else is very fond of Mozart, if not our dear Rupert?'

'Well, you can't blame him, can you?' She put a warning finger to her lips before adding quietly, 'Anyway, they could be just friendly.'

'Aye, they could. I'm not suggesting anything else at present, but I'm hoping that they get to be more than friendly, for his sake anyway.'

'Bill!'

'Well, that's what you're wishin', too, isn't it?'

'Yes, yes, I am, but' – she turned and looked along the corridor from where the sound of raised voices and laughter came – 'she'll be upset if she gets to know. I've thought that over the past year she would have grown out of him, but although she behaves herself when he's here, I'm afraid she's still got this thing about him. And, I'm sure he's sensed it because he's very tactful in that he doesn't give her any opportunity to get too close. He's either letting Mamie hang on to him or holding Angela. By the way' – her voice lightened – 'you must come and see. You know that box of plasticine that Mamie used to play with? Well, apparently she was clearing out her cupboard and she put it on the floor, and Angela toddled over to it, sat down beside it and started to play with it. I think it was the different colours that attracted her at first. That was a few days ago. I saw her squashing it in her hand and I went to take it from her, because I thought she would mess herself up. But her face started to crumple as if she was going to cry, so I left her to it. Well, about an hour ago she went to the cupboard, I wasn't in the room, but Katie said she pulled the plasticine box out, took off the lid, and picked up a piece of red plasticine and started to roll it in between her two hands. And Katie said she made a biggish ball; then a smaller ball, and then tried to stick them together. It was then that Katie came shouting for me because what Angela was trying to do

154

was copy the fat boy on the lid whose head was a round ball and his body a bigger ball. And when I got into the room there she was, looking up at me and pointing to the two plasticine balls. Willie and Sammy were there too, and apparently what Sammy had done was to roll two pieces longways to represent legs. And when he stuck them onto the body she laughed and laughed. Come and see.'

As they entered the playroom they were greeted with a chorus of, 'Hello, Dad,' and a repeat of Fiona's words, 'Come and see! Come and see what Angela's done.' But when the child put her arms around Bill's neck Fiona cried, 'Oh! your suit.'

'Who worries about a suit? How's my clever girl?'

The child, its mouth wide, said something that sounded like, 'Di . . . da.' And Bill repeated, 'Yes, Da . . . da.'

'Di . . . da. Di . . . da.'

Bill put the child down on to the floor, and she immediately went to the plasticine box and when Sammy lifted up the two balls and the legs dropped off there was much laughter and booing from the others. And he, kneeling before the child, said, 'Well, I'm not as clever as she is, am I Angie?'

The child was obviously enjoying this and she threw herself against him, her arms around his neck, and when they both fell sideways there was more laughter.

Fiona stooped down and picked up the child, thinking as she did so, Nobody's going to stop him calling her Angie now; I should have nipped it in the bud in the first place. But what odds! It was strange, though, how she always threw herself upon Sammy. With others she would put her arms around their neck and hug them tight. But always her attitude towards Sammy was this throwing of her whole self at him. Probably it was because she didn't see Sammy as often as she saw the other children. It could be the way he held her; as he had done right from the very first. He hadn't just nursed her, he had rocked her, continuously rocked her

155

until at times she had to say, 'Don't your arms ache, Sammy?'

'Why, no!' He would answer. 'Should they?'

Sammy was in his third year at the private school and she couldn't see all that improvement in him, except perhaps he had grown taller, especially in this last year. He was now the same height as Willie.

Sammy now brought Bill's attention to himself when he said, 'Well, I'll be off.'

'What d'you mean, you'll be off? You're stayin' to the tea, aren't you? Your da's comin'.'

'No; no, he's not. That's why I'm goin' home. He . . . he had to come home at dinner-time. He had a pain in his bell . . . stomach. He went and lay down. I just came round to bring Angie's present.'

'Pain in his stomach? Had he a skinful last night?'

'No; he wasn't out. He hasn't been out nights this week, not since he broke off with her, his . . . his girl-friend.'

'He's broken off with her, final, has he?'

'Aye, so he says. But she'll be after him again.'

Bill was bending down to Sammy and he said, 'He's never been out at nights at all? Is he bad? Does he look bad?'

'No, no, he doesn't look bad, but he sounds bad. He's not cussin' so much.'

'Well, hold your hand a minute. Wait downstairs; I'll run you home.'

'I've got a bike; there's no need.'

'If I remember rightly the idea was for you to stay the night and go back in the daylight; so go downstairs and wait a minute; your bike can go in the boot. I want to have a word with your da.'

Bill turned to Fiona, saying, 'It's goin' to be a family party this. Rupert, now Davey.'

Before Fiona could say anything, Katie, with a worried expression on her face jumped up, saying, 'Rupert's not coming? Why?'

'He didn't give me any reason except that he's got another engagement.'

'But he said he was coming. He always comes. I mean he comes to all our parties.'

'Yes, he does; but tonight he's got an engagement.'

'What kind of an engagement?'

Bill's voice startled them all as he yelled at her, 'I don't know, Katie, what kind of an engagement; I only know that Rupert is a man an' that he's got his own life to live an' he doesn't tell me who he's goin' to meet or what he's goin' to do with his evenings. Whether he plays ping-pong, or squash, or takes a lass out, or what have you, he hasn't got to confide in me, nor you, miss, nor anybody else in this house. So get that into your head.'

Fiona said nothing but she followed him on to the landing, and they were going down the stairs before she said, 'That was a bit thick.'

'It had to come. There'll be trouble one of these days if she doesn't wake up. You'll have to have a talk with her.'

'Oh! Bill; I've had a talk with her. She's at an awkward age. It's only time that will talk her out of it.'

'Well, all I can say is, roll on time. . . .Oh, love' – his voice dropped – 'after such a good day it's a disappointin' evenin'. But there must be something wrong with Davey for him to leave the job, and I want to find out what. I won't be long.'

As he made his way to the cloakroom at the far end of the hall the phone rang, and Fiona went towards the marble-topped, half-moon table with the bronze supports that Bill had bought with the other oddments in the house. There was a comfortable straight-backed yellow upholstered chair to the side of it, and as she sat down she picked up the phone and was half-way giving the number when the voice said, 'Fiona.'

How was it, she thought, that even her name on her mother's lips seemed to carry censure.

157

'Yes, Mother.'

'This is the third time I've tried to get through. I tried twice yesterday.'

'Well, we've been here all the time, Mother. Oh, perhaps yesterday it was so sunny we must have been out in the garden. Such a change to have such a day this time of the year.'

She was speaking in a pleasant conversational tone when her mother said, 'I have news for you.'

'Yes? I hope it's good.'

'Well, you'll likely think so, by getting rid of me.'

'Oh, Mother! Please, please, don't start. But tell me your good news, please.'

'I'm going to be married.'

Fiona paused before she said, 'Oh . . . well, I'm happy for you, Mother.' Her mind jumped to Davey – his girlfriend had left. 'Is he someone local, Mother?'

'No; he is no one local. He is an American and lives there. I'm going next week.'

'To America?'

'Yes, to America. I've been before, you know.'

'Yes, I know, but . . . but to live there.'

'Well, that should please you, dear: no more troublesome mother, no more interfering grandmother. But then I don't get much of a chance, do I? I very rarely see my grandchildren.'

'That is your fault, Mother. I've asked you numerous times to come here. I said I woud pick you up at any time you liked. But no; you couldn't bear to see the house that Bill had given me; and now apparently you never will. I suppose your future husband is one of those gentlemen you met when you were last in America?'

'Yes, he is; and I was stupid enough to spurn his attentions then.'

Spurn his attentions. Dear! dear! She hoped whoever the future husband was he would enjoy her phraseology.

158

'When are you leaving, Mother?'

'Next Tuesday.'

'As soon as that?'

'Yes, as soon as that. The house is up for sale and the funiture is to be auctioned in Newcastle. It's all in hand.'

'May I ask if your future husband is in a good position?'

'A very good position, very good. He's in what you call the real estate business. He deals with the buying and selling of big ranches, no small stuff.'

'I'm so pleased to hear that; you'll be well taken care of.'

'Yes, I'll be well taken care of, Fiona.'

'Oh, Mother.'

'It's too late, Fiona, for soft talk. You have never understood me. You have never tried. However, I suppose I'll see you before I go.'

She found it difficult to answer for a moment, and then she said, 'Yes; yes of course, Mother. I'll come over tomorrow.'

'I'll be out all day tomorrow and I'll be very busy visiting friends until next Tuesday. If you have time you can come and see me off at Newcastle Airport. As it is the last time we are likely to meet unless I decide to come back for a holiday, perhaps you could arrange to drive me to the airport? I've got to be there by eleven o'clock.'

Again she found difficulty in speaking; and then she said, 'Yes, Mother, I'll do that. I'll be there.'

'Thank you, Fiona.'

The line went dead. She replaced the phone and looked to where Bill was standing near the front door. 'I can always tell by your face when it's her,' he said.

'She's leaving. She's . . . she's going to America to be married.'

'Oh, thank God for double mercies! Now, lass, don't you be a hypocrite and say you're sorry, because she's been tangled in your hair ever since you can remember.'

159

'Oh, you don't know what I . . . well, I'm glad she's going to be married. Yes, I am. But I'm sorry for her reasons for going. She's like somebody drowning, she's clutching at straws.'

'Oh, I shouldn't worry about that side of it, lass; she'll enjoy it. She'll play the English lady to the last curtain. And you know the Americans fall over themselves for nobility. And she can ape the so-called class to a T, can your mother. Come on; come on; don't let that worry you. Face up to facts. You've never got on, never. So don't get sentimental about her goin' to America. Anyway, the way planes fly now it's like goin' across the river to North Shields.'

He kissed her; then opened the front door and, looking down the drive to where Sammy was standing with his bike, he said, 'The fact that that lad is wantin' to get home tells me there's something wrong with Davey. Anyway, I won't be long, love.' He kissed her again, then went out.

Having put Sammy's bike in the boot of the car, he said to the boy, 'Get yourself in.'

He started the car, then straightaway turned to Sammy and asked, 'Are you worried about your da?'

'Some.'

'Some a lot or some a little?'

'He's not like himself, an' he's not eatin' like he used to either, just at times.'

'Is he still drinkin'?'

'Aye, I suppose so.'

'How much?'

'He gets through two or three cans. I think he must be worryin' about his job.'

'Worryin' about his job?' Bill glanced quickly at the boy. 'What makes you think that?'

'He was dozing the other night and he woke himself yellin', "I'm as fit as the next. I can do me job."'

'Well, he's got no need to worry about his job. He's a good worker is your da.'

160

'I know that. He might be thick about some things but he's a worker.'

Again Bill glanced at him; and now his voice was harsh as he said, 'Don't call your da thick. He's no more thick than you or me.'

Sammy now turned his head slowly and looked at Bill as he said, 'If anybody was sayin' that you an' me da were alike up top, you'd want to knock their bloody . . . well *you would*, you'd want to knock their *bloody heads off.*'

Bill drew in a breath that expanded his waistcoat. He wanted to check the boy straightaway for the 'bloody', but then how could he? His father's vocabulary was made up of, bloody, buggers, and sods, nothing further, just those three words. But the lad was stuck in between the private school wallahs and his da. And it was ten to one his da would always win. However, the lad was sensible enough to tone it down when up at the house.

He made to change the subject now by saying, 'Willie tells me you're good at maths; you came out on top in the exam.'

'Anybody can do that if they can understand the computer. It's that that does it.'

'Don't be daft. Where would the computer be without your mind or anybody else's? In the long run they only do what they're told.'

Out of the blue Sammy said, 'Katie's worried. She's . . . she's upset about somethin'.'

Bill stared ahead at the two red rear lights of the car some way in front. Nothing escaped this little bloke. 'What makes you think that?' he asked.

'Well, she doesn't cry for nowt, not Katie.'

He swung the wheel round and entered the side street before he said, 'Cryin'? Katie? When was this?'

'Oh, a while back.' And then he added, 'You want to know somethin'?'

161

'Aye. Aye.'

'She's not worried about school.'

'Then why did you say she was worried?'

'I was bein' what you could call tactful and evasive.'

Tactful and evasive, he said. Put in that way he was certainly pickin' up somethin' from his private education, on one side at least.

'Well, would you mind tellin' me what you're bein' tactful and evasive about?'

'You'll bawl me out.'

'I don't see why I should as long as you're tellin' the truth and not tryin' to cause mischief.'

'I never try to cause mischief. I don't do that.'

'Samuel Love. I've warned you about barkin' at me.'

'Aye, well. And I've told you once afore an' all when you called me a liar that I didn't tell bloody lies, 'cos I wasn't afraid to speak the truth. I'm not afraid of nobody.'

'Big fella, aren't you? Big fella.'

'No. 'Cos, I've been a little fella for a long time; an' been made to face it.'

Well, the private school might be puttin' some long words into his mouth but they couldn't do much to alter that character. It had been formed a long time ago and apparently it knew all about itself. By aye, it did. He wasn't afraid of anybody because he had been little. He said now, 'Well, what's this you think that's troublin' Katie?'

'Mr Meredith.'

The wheel moved sharply under Bill's hands although he was on a straight course. 'Mr Meredith? What's he got to do with it?'

'She's got a thing about him. Always has had since I remember. An' now he's got this other lass. Well, she's not a lass, it's Miss Isherwood from along the road in the bungalow.'

'How d'you make that out?'

'I've seen them together twice. I saw them comin' out of

the pictures one day; another time I saw them goin' into the park.'

'Did you now? Did you now?' Well, there was one thing sure, Katie didn't know about this.

'What are you goin' to do about it?'

He had reached the Crescent and pulled the car to a stop. He turned and looked at Sammy and, putting his hand out and laying it on the boy's shoulder, he said, 'I can do nothin' about it, laddie. She'll have to get over it. You see, we all go through these phases. You will an' all. Oh yes, you will.' He was wondering why he was emphasising it because the boy had made no denial of what might lie before him, no protest as some boys would have done. Just as Katie was older than her years, so was this little fella. And he wasn't so little any more either, he was sproutin' all right. 'Time'll take care of it,' he said; 'she'll get over it. But she must work things out for herself. You understand? Nobdoy's goin' to enlighten her about this. D'you get me?'

'Aye, I get you. And you needn't tell me not to open me mouth.'

'No, Sammy, no, I needn't. But thanks for . . . well, for tellin' me. Not that I haven't guessed somethin' along the same lines meself; and her mother has an' all.'

'You have?'

'Oh aye, yes.'

'An' you've still done noth . . .?' He shook his head, then added, 'Well, as you say, she's got to work it out. But it's rotten.'

There was feeling in the last words as if in some way he had experienced what Katie was going through.

'Come on; out you get.'

'It's us, Da.' The boy called as soon as he opened the front door: and Davey's answering voice came from a room off the small hall: 'What's brought you back so early?'

'I had to drive Mr B into town; he was frightened of the dark.'

163

Bill laughed as he followed the boy into the sitting-room, there to see Davey pulling himself up from a low black leather chair.

'Hello, boss. What brings you here? Oh –' He pulled his neck up out of the thick sweater, saying, ''Cos I left the job?'

'Sit yourself down. What I want to know is, what took you from the job?'

As his father sat down, Sammy said, 'You had any tea, Da?'

'No, not yet. Anyway, I'm not hungry.'

'Well, you had better 'cos I'm goin' to make it; and if you don't eat it I'll throw it over you.'

As the boy walked out Davey laughed and shook his head, saying to Bill, 'See what I've got to put up with? That's what a private school does. Dear God! Havin' to pay money for that.'

'He's all right. You'll not have to worry about him, but what about you? Now, what's the matter with you?'

'Nowt, boss, really. I just had a pain in me gut, that's all . . . I'd . . . I'd been runnin' all mornin', so I thought . . . well.'

'Have you had the doctor?'

'Doctor?' Davey pulled himself further up against the back of the couch. 'Doctor? What do I want with a doctor? I've had the cramp, a bit of diarrhoea. Something I've eaten.'

'From what I hear you've had this cramp on and off for some time. And you're not eatin'.'

'Huh! That 'un' – Davey thumbed towards the door – 'he's got a mouth as big as mine already. What he'll be like when he grows up God an' His Holy Mother only knows. I tell you boss, I'm all right. I'll be back on the job the morrow.'

'You won't be back on the job the morrow. You'll get yourself to the doctor's.'

'Not me, boss; I've never been to the doctor's in me life.

164

I came into the world without one and I'll go out without one.'

'Big fella, aren't you?'

'Aye, from the head downwards.'

'What's happened to you and your lady friend?'

'Oh, we didn't see eye to eye. But truth to tell, boss, it was more Sammy an' her didn't see eye to eye. An' you know, I'd had enough of argy-bargy with the other one and I wasn't gona have it with this 'un. She had no claim on me, nor me on her for that matter. To tell you the truth, I'm glad it's ended. She was after havin' a wedding ring on her finger. Oh God Almighty! that scared me. She was all right at first, mind: anything goes; that was her attitude. Then she gets broody, lookin' at bairns in prams. It was then I saw the red light. I think I made·him' – he again pointed towards the door – 'the excuse. Anyway, you can get too much of a good thing you know.' He pulled a face. 'I must be gettin' old afore me time. And I don't know whether you've experienced it, boss, likely you have, but some women'd eat you alive, straight on without a sprinkle of salt or a dust of pepper and they wouldn't leave a bit of you for the morrow.'

'Aw, Davey.' Bill started to laugh. 'There must be somethin' radically wrong with you if your night life's gone astray.'

'Aye, I thought that meself, boss, I thought that meself. Aye I did. God's truth I did.'

'Aw, Davey.'

'What d'you really think of the young 'un, boss, I mean your real opinion?'

'What do I think of Sammy? I think he's a fine lad. And I'll tell you something else, I envy you, that you've got a son like him. That's not to say I don't love my youngster, I more than love her, but there are times when . . . well you know what I mean, as one to another a man thinks of a son. He knows he's goin' to die some day but in a son he'll live again, more so than in a daughter. You know what I mean?'

'Aye, boss.' Davey was looking into the fire now. 'Aye, I know what you mean about livin' again in your son. But I hope he makes a better job of his life than I have 'cos what have I done with it? The only peak I've reached is two court appearances and land meself up in jail, not forgettin' me hundred hours community work. Let's hope he does better than that.'

What could he say? It was quite true; that's all Davey had done with his life. Yet, on the other hand, he made people happy. Usually he had only to open his mouth and he caused laughter. And so he was forced to say, 'That might be so, Davey, but on the other hand you've caused a lot of fun in your time. You've made people laugh who didn't know how to. And don't forget, most of all, you fathered Sammy.'

The door was pushed open and Sammy entered, carrying a tray. He started straightaway: 'It's nice boiled ham and you like cold sausages,' he said. 'I've cut the bread and butter thin.' And turning to Bill, he said, 'I've brought you a cup of tea an' all.'

'Thanks, Sammy. That'll be welcome, that's if it's strong.'

'Aye, it's strong. I stuck a knife in it and it didn't fall over.'

'You'll get your ears clipped me lad' – his father was nodding at him – 'with your smart alec answers.'

Bill now watched Davey look down on the plate, then look at his son and say, 'Now I'll have that with a glass of beer in a little while, but I'll enjoy the tea. How many sugars did you put in?'

'The usual. I should know by now, shouldn't I?'

'You see what I've got to put up with? That's what a private school does for you. Begod! He's comin' away from there, and soon.'

Bill and Sammy exchanged knowing glances, and when

166

Davey had finished his tea and lay back against the head of the couch, conversation became a little strained; and so Bill rose, saying, 'Well, now, I'm not expectin' to see you the morrow or the next day. You get to the doctor's in the mornin'.'

'We'll see.'

'No, we'll see; if it's diarrhoea he'll give you something for it.'

'Well, that's all it is. I know me inside. But thanks, boss, for comin'.' His voice dropped. 'I'm grateful. I'm always grateful to you and your family, always: for one big reason at least, and you know what that is. Good-night to you.'

'Good-night, Davey.'

At the door Bill, bending down to Sammy, said, 'Don't you go to school the morrow; see that he gets to the doctor's, d'you hear?'

'Aye. Aye, I hear. But it's easier said than done. He'll likely turn up for work.'

'If he does then I'll send him back. Anyway do your best.' He ruffled the boy's hair, then went out. . . .

At home Fiona met him in the hall. 'How did you find him?' she said.

'To tell the truth I don't know. He says he's got diarrhoea, but from what that lad says he hasn't been eatin', and for some time, and he doesn't go out at nights. And you should see him, the look of him; I'd like to bet it's somethin' more than diarrhoea.'

'Has he been to the doctor?'

'No; and it's going to take an explosion to get him there; he's never been to a doctor in his life apparently. He hadn't one to bring him into the world, he says, and he's not goin' to have a one to see him out of it. I don't like it.' He took her arm and walked her across the hall and into the long drawing-room. 'It's odd, don't you think, how he and that lad have got under me skin, under all our skins. I suppose

167

it's because they're laughter makers. But like all laughter makers there's another side to them. And I saw that side the night, and it saddened me: it was as if I too was picking up the other side of them, the lonely lost side. . . .Oh! as Davey himself would say, let's stop mummerin' and have a drink. Come on with you.'

2

It was Boxing Day, as Bill put it, wet squib day. All the excitement of Christmas Day was over. They were eating the little remains of a turkey, a leg of pork, and a ham. Yesterday had been acclaimed a grand day by all concerned: the family, and those now considered to be part of it Nell and Bert, and Rupert, and Sammy, and the visitors: Davey, who apparently was much better in health, and Miss Isherwood. But today the family were scattered about the house, following their own pursuits.

Bill and Bert were playing snooker in the games room; Mark was up in what had been turned into his own bedroom-cum-study, one of the attics; in another room under the roof Willie and Sammy were deep into the intricacies of a computer that Willie had been given for his Christmas Box; Mamie was curled up on the playroom couch admiring her gold charm bangle as she twisted it round her wrist; while in the third attic, which was still used as a lumber room, Katie stood at the window from which, through the bare trees, she had a distant glimpse of the road that led past the grounds and the bungalow on the outskirts of the paddock.

Downstairs in the drawing-room, seated each side of the

fireplace, were Nell and Fiona, and the baby Angela was asleep on the couch where it faced the fireplace.

Nell was bending forward, her hands clasped on her knees; 'I've got to tell you, Fiona,' she was saying; 'I've been putting it off and off. I've fallen pregnant.'

'Oh! Nell.' Fiona got straight up from her seat and caught Nell's hands and said, 'Oh, I am glad for you, I am. I am. Why . . . why didn't you tell me? Why couldn't you tell me?'

Nell didn't glance towards the couch, but there lay the reason. As she had said to Bert, she wasn't afraid of having a child like Angela, but she was afraid of its being so normal that it would upset Fiona, probably a wedge between them. So she couldn't give any explanation except to say, 'I . . . I don't know now why I didn't.' Yet, even as she spoke the words Fiona knew the reason for her reticence. And she said, 'Oh, Nell, Nell. I want you to have a child. Even if she was like Angela I would still wish you to have it. But it'll be all right. And Bert, what does he say?'

'Well, remember how Bill took it when you told him? Somehow similar, he just couldn't believe it. Then he got all worked up and frightened that something would happen to me and began to talk about my age and so on and so on. But inside he's delighted.'

'Bill'll knock his block off for keeping it to himself, you'll see.' Fiona bent down now and, pulling Nell up to her, she put her arms round her and kissed her, saying, 'When is it due?'

'July, early I should say.'

'Oh, come on; let's go and tell Bill.' She picked up the sleeping child from the couch, 'I'll put her in her cot.'

As they went up the main staircase Katie was running down the back staircase and letting herself out of the side door. She was wearing her old school coat but had a large scarf round her neck and a woollen hat on. She did not make for the drive but crossed the yard by the stable block, went through the arch that led to the vegetable garden, then on down through the shrubbery and the orchard until she came to the paddock. The paddock had once been the grazing ground of Sir Roger Oliver's horses, and so she kept to the perimeter of it as she knew it was muddy in the middle. At the row of cypresses and the low wall that marked the boundary of the estate she bent down and crept between the boles of the trees.

Leaning over the wall she looked at the cottage just a few yards to the right, and at the newer part built on to it and known as the bungalow. On the road outside stood a car, Rupert's car. She had guessed it was when she had seen it from the attic window. And it wasn't the first time she had seen it there, and it had no right to be there; not now, because yesterday he had been nice to her, ever so nice. When they were playing games he had chosen her and not that lanky Miss Isherwood. She hated her; she acted as if she knew everything just because she had lived here all her life. And what was more, she was two-faced: she had made believe she liked Mr Love; she had chosen him twice. And when the games-room floor had been cleared for dancing and everybody tried to do the Gay Gordons, she had hung on to Mr Love; she had even leant her head on his shoulder when she laughed so much; and when he had sung a funny Irish song she had clapped like anything. She was two-faced, she was horrible.

It took but a minute to get over the wall and to the back door of the cottage. To the left was a small window.

Standing close by the door she thought she heard voices; then she was sure when she heard someone laugh. She bit hard on her lip. He was in there talking to her, laughing with her. Well, there was nothing to stop her from calling, was there? She could say that she had seen his car and her mother wondered if he was coming to tea. . . .No, she had better not say that; she had better not mention her mother's name. She woud just say, quite ordinary like, 'I wondered

171

if you were coming to tea.' Yes, that's what she would do. She would just walk in. She would go round the front and ring the bell. She had never been in the bungalow but her presence would stop them doing whatever they were doing, talking or laughing, or. . . .

Before the thought had time to clarify she heard the laughter again, and instinctively her hand went out to the iron latch on the door. What she meant to do was to rattle it to get their attention, but when she lifted the latch the door swung open and disclosed a small room and in the middle of it a narrow bed. And now from the bed there, looking at her, were two startled faces.

She did not turn and run; nor was she aware of taking two steps into the room; but almost at the moment the man cried, 'Katie! Go away,' her foot kicked something. She looked down. Two wooden things lying to the side of her feet. One was an old-fashioned wooden pestle bowl, about eight inches deep, the other was the pestle itself. Some part of her mind noted it was just like a potato pounder. She wasn't aware that she had stooped and picked them up, but when they were in her hands she knew she was yelling, 'You're filthy! Horrible. Dirty. I hate you!'

She noticed the form of arc the bowl flew in after leaving her hand; then there was a scream and the woman was sitting up holding her head. She had no clothes on. And now as she let the other implement fly from her hand she saw him about to throw the bedclothes back and she heard the dull thud as it caught him on the side of his face; and the next minute, there he was, stark naked, and he had her by the shoulders and he was shaking her.

His hand came out: first on one side of her face and then on the other, and the second blow knocked her flying against the small dressing-table.

He had hold of her again and was dragging her to her feet and through her swimming senses she glimpsed the woman now sitting on the edge of the bed: she was moaning and

172

her face was covered with blood; his face too was all blood.

She screamed as his hand gripped her hair and swung her around and threw her towards the door. The next thing she knew she was on her hands and knees on a rough gravel path and she was crying aloud.

She struggled to her feet but could not see the way to go because the tears were blinding her and her head was spinning and her ears were still ringing and both sides of her face hurt. She wasn't really aware of tumbling over the wall or getting up or groping her way through trees. And she didn't return round the perimeter of the paddock but went straight across it, her shoes squelching in the boggy part, and the mud coming over the tops of them.

When she eventually staggered through the kitchen and into the passage that led to the dining-room and met the four adults coming out of the games room, only then did she come to a stop; and they stared at her in blank amazement as she gasped, 'He hit m . . . me. He's filthy! Dirty! And he hit . . . me.'

'Oh my God! What's . . . what's happened? You're all blood, girl. Who hit you? Who hit you?' Bill had hold of her now.

'He did. Rupert. He's filthy. He had nothing on, nothing, and he got hold of me. . . .And she had nothing on, nothing!' She was yelling now. 'But I hit them. I hit them both. Her face is all blood. . . .'

Bill was now almost dragging her along the passage, and Fiona at her other side was gabbling, 'Why did you go there? What made you? What have you done?' Tell me! Tell me!'

In the drawing-room Bill pushed her onto a chair and, bending over her, said, 'Let's get this straight. You went along to the bungalow and you saw Rupert and Miss Isherwood in bed. *Is that it? Is that it?*' He was screaming at her now, and she was still spluttering, 'They . . . they had nothing on. Nothing.'

173

Bill stood back from her and raised his hand and cried, 'For two pins I'd knock you from here to hell, girl!'

'Bill! Bill! Go and see what's happened. Please!'

It seemed that he didn't hear her, for he stood glaring down on the distraught girl, but then swinging round he hurried from the room, and Katie muttered, 'Mam. Mam, my face hurts, and my knees. Look!'

Fiona looked at her daughter's knees. Her stockings were torn; there was blood oozing through the dust coating them, but she made no comment.

Nell said quietly now, 'I'd better get a dish of water;' but then, turning to Bert, she said, 'No; you go and get it. Get a bowl from the kitchen and a flannel from the bathroom;' she had seen Fiona press her hand tightly across her mouth: 'Come and sit down,' she said.

'Oh Nell, what if she's. . . .'

'We don't know what she's done. Just sit down.'

'I know what I did,' Katie said, '*I hit her.* I hit them both.'

'What did you hit them with?' It was Nell asking the question, and in a cool voice.

'It hit her anyway, the bowl, right in the face.'

'You're a wicked girl; you know that?'

'I don't care. He shouldn't have done it. He has a wife in an asylum. He could have had me; he didn't need to ask. *Yes, he could. Yes, he could.*' She was now bending forward, her head and hands wagging. And Nell and Fiona looked at each other, before concentrating again on Katie. Here was a girl not yet fourteen saying that this man, who could have been her father, could have her for the asking. She was saying, 'He didn't need to ask.'

As Nell was asking herself, 'What's the world coming to?' Fiona was almost whimpering, 'Oh my God! And she's my daughter.' She had always thought that drug taking by any of them would have broken her up. To her mind there was nothing worse, but she had been proved wrong. Why had life to be like this? Why had growing to be so painful? It

174

had always been painful for the young. But now, this brashness, this blatant offering of herself . . . of her daughter's self. . . .

Down the road Rupert was saying to Bill much the same thing at this moment. 'Bill, I'm telling you, something will have to be done with that girl or you're going to have trouble. I've been patient; I've tried all ways. Come on, dear.' He now led the young woman towards the door. She was holding a large pad of cotton wool over her brow, and Bill said, 'Let me have a look.'

'No, no.' She gently pressed him away.

'It's just missed her eye. My God! That child! That girl is mad. Just imagine if it had been her eye. As for me, her aim wasn't so straight.' He dabbed at the still bleeding cut on his chin.

'Where are you going?' Bill asked quietly.

'I'm taking her to the hospital; it will have to be stitched.'

'I'm sorry, Rupert. I'm sorry you've been put through this. By God! I'll take the skin off her hide when I get back.'

'I shouldn't bother. Her face won't be bleeding tomorrow but it will be showing the imprints of my hands, both sides, and her back likely too, because I knocked her flying. I . . . I could have killed her. Do you know that?'

'How did she get in?'

'The cottage door was open. I'd been out that way to get some logs for the fire. I never thought about locking it, not till later on.' His words now coming between his teeth, he added, 'We didn't expect a visitor.'

He locked the door now, the door of the bungalow; then taking the young woman's arm, he said, 'All right, Caroline, come on. Come on, dear,' and led her to the car.

Having settled her and put a rug over her knees, he turned to Bill, saying, 'She's spoilt a good friendship. You understand?'

'Yes. Yes, Rupert, I understand. And I'm sorry. But it needn't make any difference between us. And for goodness

175

sake! don't let it cut you off from the house altogether. Fiona and the others would miss you.'

'It will be impossible to call now. You know that, Bill.'

'There's always the daytime when they're at school.'

'We'll see. We'll see.'

Bill watched the car being driven away. There was mingling in him a feeling of loss and that he must vent his rising anger. But he did not hurry back to the house; and when he entered it, he took off his coat very slowly. He had gone out without a cap. Then his steps still slow, he made his way into the drawing-room.

Fiona and Nell turned towards him, but not Katie. Nell had just finished bathing Katie's knees and the palms of her hands; and as Bill approached she picked up the bowl and put it to one side, and Fiona, rising quickly from the couch, said, 'Bill. Wait; wait.'

'What for?' He looked at her. 'Until she decides to come into our room and split my head open because I'm in bed with you?'

'*Bill. Please!*'

He pressed her aside, not roughly but very firmly; then bending over Katie, he hauled her up by the shoulders and he held her there as he stared into her deepening red face, saying now, 'I only wish at this minute that I was your real father, and you know what I would do? I would strip you naked and I would take the buckle end of a belt to you. Today you've not only almost blinded a woman, and might have done the same to a man, but you've broken a good friendship. You spoilt something that I valued, and your mother valued, and it'll take a long, long, time to live it down. We're supposed to be in a modern age, and yet what I still want to do is to lift me hand and swipe you to the other end of the room, and out of it, miles away. But Rupert's done that, hasn't he? And it's showing. You know something else? You should be ashamed of yourself the way you've thrown yourself at that fella. No man ever respects a

176

woman, nor does a lad respect a girl who's cheap. And you've made yourself the cheapest of the cheap this day. Now' – he pointed at her – 'while I can remain calm, at least in some control of meself, get yourself out of me sight. An' don't expect any kindness from me for a long, long, time. Go on!' He swung her round and thrust her forward, and she ran from him sobbing, like a young girl again and not as Fiona had seen her a short while ago almost like, as her mind had told her, a potential young prostitute.

As Fiona dropped into a chair she said, 'How did you find them?'

'It's how the hospital finds her. She's got a split above her eyebrow. Rupert says it's two inches long. The thing just missed her eye. And he's got a split chin.'

'She said he hit her.'

'Yes, he did, gentleman Rupert. And if I'd been him I wouldn't have stopped at where *he* stopped at just slapping her face and throwing her out, I'd have blacked her eyes. You understand what she's done, don't you? She's put an end to a good relationship? What's to be done with her?'

Fiona looked at him and shook her head slowly as she said, 'Nothing, except what she does to herself, and that will be punishment enough. What's happened will put an end to a phase that we all go through, only hers is finished long before its time. He had become an obsession with her, and she shouldn't have had to experience that at this age. But now it's over and, if I'm not mistaken, and I hope I'm not, it'll put her off the male sex for a long time.'

'You don't say.'

'Oh, Bill, please don't take it like that. I'm just trying to put myself in her place. Anyway, your promised attitude towards her in the future will be punishment enough, for you came next in line to him. Anyway' – she moved from him now – 'I'd better go and warn the others to leave her alone.'

When she left the room Bill turned to Nell and said,

177

'What d'you make of it, Nell? Eh? What d'you make of it?' And before she could answer he added, 'And there's you bringing another one into the world. You must be mad. People don't know what they're askin' for when they crave for a family. I was once a middle of the road man with not a care in the world: as long as I got plenty to eat and drink an' I was in work an' a bit of pleasure on the side, that was life. And look what I landed meself with.'

'You wouldn't have it otherwise, would you?'

'Ah Nell, I sometimes wonder, more so a few minutes ago down the road when I saw one of the nicest fellas in the world, a real gentleman, bespattered with blood and tellin' me that he had been brought to such a pitch that he knocked a young lass about and had thrown her bodily into the road; and that the close, warm association he had with us all in this house had to come to an end. It was then I knew, Nell, that I would have had it otherwise. Oh aye, I would have had it otherwise.'

PART FOUR

THE THIRD BIRTHDAY

1

'What do you make of it, Doctor? Now just look at that.'
Bill picked up a piece of plasticine that had been roughly
shaped into a face and, pointing, he said, 'There's two holes
for the eyes but there's no hole for the nose. The nose has
been built up you see. And look at that. Look at the mouth;
then look at mine.'

Doctor Pringle nodded while smiling and he said, 'Yes;
yes, you're right. As you say, the nose is built up and it's a
pretty big one; it's like yours except it's a bit outsize.'

'Which d'you mean, the plasticine one or mine?'

'Oh, we'll say the plasticine one.'

'And look, the piece underneath's representing the body:
it's pressed in from what are the shoulders. And there's the
buttons on the waistcoat.'

Bill now pointed to his own waistcoat.

'Yes, it is remarkable. And you say she did this all herself?'

'Aye. She's done others an' all. Now there's nothing
wrong with her mind when she can do that, is there?'

'No; you're right. I don't think there's anything wrong
with her mind as far as it goes.'

'What d'you mean, not as far as it goes?'

'Well, let's say that her brain won't turn her into a scientist or a mathematician.'

'Well, there's not all that many of them knockin' about, is there?'

'No; you're right there too; comparatively few against the whole population. But we know that there'll be limitations in Angela's case. She's made remarkable progress as it is: she's walking and talking and is a delightful child altogether. But I think you know that her mental capacity won't go beyond six or seven. You already know that, don't you?'

'I've been told that, but I don't believe it, not with her. And look at that.'

He again pointed to the plasticine model. 'She started last year by rolling two balls together. Now, and she's not yet three, you show me any other bairn of her age that can do that, make a kind of likeness. Have you got one on your books that can do it?'

'No, no. I can't recall any child at the moment. So we can say she has a special gift, and if she develops it, who knows, she could be a sculptor.'

'Aye. Aye, she could.' Bill looked down on the model and muttered, 'She was special from the minute I held her' – he turned and glanced at the doctor – 'when I got over the first shock, because you tell me anybody in a similar situation who doesn't get a shock.'

'No; that's quite natural; and as you say she's special.' The doctor did not add what he was thinking, special to you if to no one else.

They both turned as Fiona came into the room and she, looking towards the low table where the plasticine lay in blobs, said, 'Is he boring you to death, doctor?'

'No, no not at all. I'm finding it very interesting.' He pointed down to the moulded head, and Fiona looked at it, too, but made no remark. Bill had a thing about the child's ability with the clay. Granted she kept plying it into all shapes, but she herself didn't see any resemblance to Bill in

182

that piece, nor did she think that the child put the nose on: likely one of the others helped but they wouldn't say because they too wanted to imagine that she had some gift. More than once she had asked herself why she didn't go along with it, and the answer she always got from the first was that she wasn't going to build up any fairy tales about her little daughter. If she continued to progress as she was she would be grateful without imagining that she would one day be an artist.

The doctor turned to her now and, smiling, said, 'I think Mamie will live.' And at this she smiled too. 'She has a cold on her chest. Just keep her indoors as I said for a few days. By the way, I haven't visited you for some months now, so you must be a very healthy family. I haven't heard how your friend Nell is. Has she had her baby?'

'Oh yes' – Fiona nodded – 'and as you would say, a bonny bouncing boy. They're over the moon. Talk about doting parents.'

'Well, that's as it should be.'

As they went out of the room Fiona said to herself, Yes, that's as it should be. She was happy for Nell. Oh yes she was. But at the same time she knew she would never forget the first time she looked down on Andrew, as he was named. The tears had welled up in her and almost choked her. But it had passed. Thank God, yes, it had passed.

As they reached the bottom of the stairs Bill was saying, 'Sorry we've had to drag you out on a Saturday afternoon,' when he was interrupted by Mark turning from the telephone table, his hand over the mouthpiece of the phone, saying, 'It's a call from America, Mam.'

She exchanged a quick glance with Bill, then went and took the phone from Mark.

'Hello.'

'Will you take a call from a Mrs Vidler from the United States?'

'Yes. Oh yes.'

183

As she waited she thought, Mrs Vidler. Surely by now it should be Mrs Benson. She had had only three letters from her mother in all these months, in fact in almost a year.

Then she heard a voice as if it was coming from the other room, saying, 'Fiona?'

'Yes. Yes, Mother. How are you?'

'Fiona.'

'Yes, I can hear you, Mother.'

'I'm . . . I'm coming home.'

She paused. 'You are? For a holiday?'

'No, no; I'm coming home for good. Do . . . do you think you could meet me? I . . . I am due in Newcastle about six o'clock in the evening your time next Thursday.'

'Are you all right, Mother?'

'Yes, yes, I'm all right, dear. I . . . I will explain everything when I see you.'

Fiona held the mouthpiece and looked at it. The voice was her mother's and yet not her mother's. 'I'll . . . I'll have to go now, dear. You'll be there?'

'Yes, yes of course, Mother. I'll . . . I'll look forward to seeing you.' She didn't know whether or not she meant those words, she only knew that there was something not right. There must be something not right because she was coming home and not on a holiday, and she was still Mrs Vidler.

'Goodbye, dear.'

'Goodbye, Mother.'

She put the phone down. There was only Mark in the hall now. She looked at him and said quietly, 'It's your grandma, she's . . . she's coming back.'

He pursed his lips and said, 'Phew! more trouble.'

'Yes, perhaps, but she sounded different.'

'I couldn't imagine Gran being different, ever.'

Katie entered the hall now from the direction of the kitchen, and it was Mark who said to her, 'Granma's coming back.'

184

'Why?'

The question was directed at Fiona, and Fiona shook her head and said, 'You know as much as I do. She just said she was coming back, and not for a holiday, for good.'

At this her daughter just lifted her shoulders slightly, then turned and went up the stairs and Fiona stood for a moment looking after her. The girl had grown apace in the last year but there was none of the old sprightly Katie about her any more; very little conversation; in fact, it was almost nil. Her answers: yes, no, perhaps, why? Strangely, the only one with whom she conducted any form of conversation was Sammy; and that indeed was strange because she had always considered him, in her own jargon, common.

Thinking of Sammy reminded her that he hadn't been for two to three days, and that was unusual. She could understand his not coming over at nights but she couldn't remember a Saturday for years now when the boy hadn't been here some part of the day. That's why Willie had gone on his bike to see him.

She called now up the stairs to where Katie was disappearing along the landing: 'Look in on Mamie, will you dear?' she said.

Although she expected no response she knew that her daughter would do what she asked. It wasn't that she had become docile, but since that dreadful affair last Boxing Day when she thought she was going to have a defiant sex-ridden girl on her hands, practically the opposite had happened. Katie had become quiet, obedient, but withdrawn into herself, different. In fact the whole house had become different since Rupert no longer popped in. Only Bill saw him.

One thing that incident had done, it made Rupert take a decisive step in his own life. Within a month, Miss Isherwood had sold the bungalow and taken up her abode with him as his common law wife, and they now lived above the garage. She hadn't seen the young woman but Bill said she had a scar running along the top of her left eye that she would probably never get rid of and it was a miracle that she had the eye at all.

It pained her to see Bill's attitude to Katie: he spoke to her but he never touched her or made a fuss of her like he used to. And there were times when she would catch her daughter looking at him with a mixture of bitterness and sadness in her face. When he had first come on to their horizon she had loved him and vied for his attention; and he had given it to her. But now no more. . . .

It was only a matter of minutes later that Willie, almost throwing his bike against the house wall, ran indoors, crying, 'Mam! Dad! Dad!'

To his calling Fiona came out of the dining-room and Bill from the study along the passage.

'What is it? What is it?'

Willie stood gasping as he looked from one to the other: 'It's . . . it's Mr Davey, he's bad.'

'What d'you mean, he's bad?'

'Sammy's worried. His dad's got to go into hospital.'

'When did all this happen? He was at work yesterday.'

'Yes, yes, he was, but you said yourself last night, Dad, that you thought there was something wrong with him because the flesh was dropping off him and he shouldn't have been there.'

'Aye. Aye, I did. Well, I'd better go and see what all this is about. There's no rest for the wicked. It's likely the diarrhoea again. I've told him for months now he should go and have that seen to. But he gave it some fancy name, diverticular or something.'

Fiona nodded. 'Yes, yes, he did, diverticulitis. That can cause diarrhoea, so he said. And he was taking some medicine for it, wasn't he?'

'Maybe; but he should see the doctor. Get me coat.' He stumped along the passage, and Fiona immediately went across the hall and into the cloakroom and brought his coat

186

and soft hat to him; and as he put them on he said, 'There's always something. But I've told that idiot to get a doctor, not to rely on what somebody else told him to get.'

'The doctor came this morning. Sammy wouldn't listen any longer to his dad and he went out and phoned, and the doctor came, said he would get a bed for him by Monday,' Willie put in.

As Bill made for the door he said, 'Well, this is another of those days: Mamie coughin' her heart out, your granny comin' home and now this.'

About twenty minutes later Bill drew the car up in front of the bungalow in Primrose Crescent, and when Sammy opened the door to him Bill's voice was quiet as he said, 'How is he, lad?'

'He's bad, Mr B, real bad. He's been real bad for a long time, but you can't do anything with him, he's so pig-headed.'

Bill went slowly into the bedroom. Davey was in bed. His face looked ashen but his smile was as wide as ever and he greeted Bill with, 'I'll break that little bugger's neck. I will, so help me. Haulin' you out on a Saturday afternoon.'

'You know what you are, Davey Love, you're a bloody fool, as the youngster said, and a pig-headed one into the bargain. What is it all about?'

'Aw, well, boss, just one of those things.'

'Come off it, Davey. What is it?'

Davey looked towards the door. 'He'll be makin' tea. I'm full up to here with tea.' He tapped his forehead. 'If he's made it once the day he's made it a dozen times.'

'Never mind that. What's wrong. D'you know?'

'Oh aye, boss, I know. Aye, I know.' The smile slid from Davey's face. He looked down over the quilt before adding, 'I've know for a long time. It's what they're callin' the big C.'

Bill said nothing, he just stared down on this big rough Irishman for whom he had developed a very warm liking

187

amounting to affection. And after a long moment he said,
'And you've done nowt about it?'

'Aw, aye. Yes, I've done something about it. I've taken
things. Been to Mass.' Now the grin reappeared. 'I had a
talk with Him' – and he glanced upwards – 'but He's in two
minds where to send me: bad lads, He said, with good
intentions are difficult to place.'

'Oh, for God's sake! Davey, stop jokin' about it.'

'What d'you expect me to do, boss? Eh? I've had to make
up me mind I must face it. I've covered it up from the
youngster this long while. I've always sworn at him, but
God forgive me I've sworn at him more these last few months
than I've done since he was born.' He again looked towards
the door. 'That's the only thing I'm worryin' about, boss,
him. He'll have to go to his granny's. I mean, for good.'

'For God's sake! man, there's cures the day.'

'Aw, aye, yes, I know that, boss. God's good to a lot of
folk. But I've known from the start me number's been written
down and when it's called out I'll have to jump to it, saying,
"Present, Sir!" But seriously, boss, I'd like to thank you and
the missis 'cos you've been kindness itself to the lad. You've
shown him another side of life. So could I ask you, boss,
that when he's with the old girl you would now and again,
when you have a minute, give him a helpin' hand?'

'Shut up! Will you! You know without sayin' or askin'
that the helpin' hand will be there. An' another thing, I'll
promise you this, he won't go to his granny's 'cos he
can't stand her. Up till this week or so he's practically lived
at our house anyway. I should send you a bill for his
meals.'

'Aye, you're right there, boss. Funny, I've often thought
about that. You know, about him an' Willie, they're more
like brothers than Willie an' Mark, aren't they?'

'Yes. Yes, that's true.'

'An' they couldn't be two more opposite types, could they
now? Your lad bein' nicely spoken an' mine with a tongue

like a guttersnipe. And I'm to blame for that. Aye, I'm to blame for that. He's had a rough haul, has the youngster. But life's been different for him since he met up with Willie an' your family. An' boss, you meant that, I know you did, that you'll see to him, and that's all I want to know; I'll be ready any minute now 'cos that's settled me mind.'

'Stop talkin' bloody rot! Are you goin' to have an operation?'

'Aye, that's what he said. I go in on Monday.'

'Well, that could be the beginning of your cure. And look at it that way, sort of mind over matter. They're doin' a lot of that stuff the day. Look at me for instance. I'm a case of mind over matter. I thought I was a big shot when I was nowt; but look at me the day, sittin' pretty. So use that napper of yours. Tell yourself you're goin' to get better.'

'Just as you say, boss, just as you say.'

'I brought you some tea.'

They both looked to where Sammy was coming into the room holding a tray on which there were two cups of tea, a bowl of sugar and a plate of biscuits.

'Thanks, lad. That's just what I could do with.' Bill pulled up a chair to the side of the bed, then, looking at Sammy, he said, 'Your da tells me he's goin' in on Monday.'

'Aye, and not afore time. Pig-headed galoot!'

As Sammy turned away Davey heaved himself up in the bed and, addressing himself to Bill, said, 'D'you see what I mean? Goes to a private school an' speaks to his father in that fashion. Pig-headed galoot. Would you allow Willie to speak to you like that, I ask you? Now, would you?'

'Well, he mightn't use the same words but I often get looks that speak louder than words. Aye, I do.'

As Bill drank the strong tea he looked at the man in the bed and he found it difficult to know what to say, so he talked of the family: Mamie's cold, sending for the doctor, Angela's clever way with plasticine. And lastly he asked him had he ever seen anybody with such a permanent grin on

189

his face as was on Bert's since he had become a father: 'There's no gettin' a word in,' he said, 'not even edgeways. All he can talk about is the bairn. You'd think it was the first one that had ever been born. I think he was for usin' his fists on me, an' him the good quiet, religious, man, just 'cos I laughingly said that the bairn's mouth was a little outsize. It was yawnin' at the time. He didn't like it. You don't dare joke about his son.'

'He's a good man is Bert. He pops in now and again.'

'He does?' said Bill in surprise. 'Why the hell didn't he tell me?'

'Why should he now? You've got enough on your shoulders. And anyway, as Bert said, you're like a kangaroo hoppin' from one place to another; you were difficult to pin down. An' that's understandable 'cos this is some job you've pulled off this time, boss. By God! it is that.'

'Kangaroo hoppin' from one place to another! Just you wait till I see him. Well' – he got to his feet – 'I've got to be goin'. But listen. I'll be along the morrow, and the missis an' all. And don't worry about the lad; let your mind rest there.' He bent over and looked into the gaunt bony face as he said softly, 'You're goin' to get better. Get that into your head. Do a little talkin' to the Holy Mother that you're always callin' on and see what she can do for you.'

'Aye, I'll do that. Yes, I'll do that, boss. An' if anybody can fix it she will.' Then his smile sliding, he put out his hand and gripped Bill's, saying, 'I can rest easy now.'

At the door all Bill could say to the boy was 'We'll be over the morrow, but pack a case for Monday, you're comin' with us.'

And all Sammy said, was, 'Aye. Ta.'

Davey had his operation on the Wednesday morning. He was wheeled into the theatre at half-past nine and was wheeled out at half-past twelve. And it was four o'clock in the afternoon when Bill spoke to the surgeon; he then drove

190

straight home, went to the drinks cabinet and poured himself out two good fingers of whisky.

Standing by his side, Fiona said, 'Bad?'

'Couldn't be worse. They just sewed him up again. The surgeon said there was nothing they could do; if they had tried he would have died on the table. It was all over his body. God! what he must have been goin' through all these months. The bloody fool.'

'What's going to happen now to him?'

'He'll be in hospital for a time, and then, well . . .' He walked away from her and, standing in front of the fire, he placed his glass on the marble mantelshelf, then gripped the edge of it with both hands as he said, 'He'll need lookin' after. I'm goin' to bring him here for what time he's got left; he can't stay in that bungalow by himself.' Turning sharply towards her now, he said, 'I'll engage a nurse.'

'No, Bill, no; you needn't do that. Whatever's to be done, Nell and I can do it between us, and be only too glad. If things get very bad, all right, we'll have a nurse; but wait and see what has to be done first.'

He drew in a long breath, saying, 'I said all that without consultin' you in any way. Sorry. That's how I feel. I mean, he's a big Irish galoot, as Sammy's always tellin' him, but he's brought more laughs into this house than any comedian you see on the screen. An' the lad an' all. They somehow became linked up with the family, you know what I mean?'

'Oh yes, Bill, I know what you mean. I feel the same, and I wouldn't be able to rest if I thought he was in that bungalow all day on his own.'

He put his arms out and drew her to him, then said, 'And your mother's comin' the morrow. Things never happen singly in this house, do they? Are you worried? I mean about her coming?'

'Yes; yes, I am. There was always a dread when I used to lift the phone that I would hear her say my name, Fi . . .

191

o . . . na, drawn out, just like that. Condemnation in each syllable. I kept thinking about it last night.'

'Well' – he now gripped her shoulders – 'there's one thing I can tell you, I'm going to put me foot down straightaway when she enters that door. I don't care if I vex or please her but I'll make it plain that she's not goin' to upset you again in any way, And. . . .Oh my God! I've just thought, will we have to put her up?'

'Oh, I shouldn't think so, she'll go to an hotel.'

'Yes; yes, that would be more like her, 'cos she wouldn't want to come in close proximity to me, would she?' He smiled now, saying, 'You've never noticed or remarked recently on my use of the big words. You should hear me at the board meetings; I astonish meself.'

'Oh! Bill, Bill; you sound like your old self again.'

'Aye.' He turned from her now and picked up the glass from the mantelshelf, saying, 'We've all got old selves, haven't we? I wish I could have kept mine with regard to one person in this house.'

'You still haven't forgiven her?'

'Oh, I suppose I've forgiven her, but somehow things have never been the same, have they? She's not the same to me, naturally, and I'm not the same to her. An' none of you see Rupert except me; and you used to like him poppin' in and out, didn't you? He gave a bit of class to the place.' He wrinkled his face at her and she said, 'He was just himself, like Sir Charles used to be: they're at ease in any company. They didn't treat me or you any differently from anyone else. Except on last Boxing Day.'

'My God in heaven! I'll never forget that day as long as I live. And that's what I see every time I look at Katie, I see him and that lass bleedin' an' know that she did it, and worse, was capable of doin' it. Ah well, there's more serious things to hand now. Where will you put Davey? In the annexe?'

'No, no; that's too cut off. There's two spare bedrooms

192

up there. We'll put him in the one looking on to the drive. He'll see the comings and goings from there, that's if he's bedridden all the time.'

'Aye, that's an idea.' Again he turned and put the glass on the mantelshelf; then, pulling her to him once more, he kissed her hard on the mouth before saying, 'You're a good lass, you know. Wonderful, wonderful. And at this minute I could believe in Davey's God and thank Him for you.'

2

Fiona watched the plane taxi to a stop. She watched the doors open and the passengers come down the steps. Then she saw her mother, having recognised her more by her walk than anything else. But when a few minutes later they came face to face Fiona had trouble in hiding the shock she felt.

When she had last seen her mother, the result of the face-lift had given her a false youthfulness, but now, although the skin appeared still tight, she was definitely looking at an elderly woman, not someone just turned sixty. She was further surprised when her mother's arms went about her and her voice murmured, 'Fiona. Oh! Fiona.'

'Are . . . are you all right, Mother?'

'Yes, yes dear; I'm all right, only tired. I've had a long journey, even before I got on the plane. And then there were the changes and –' She sighed before adding, 'How are you, dear?'

'Oh, I'm fine, Mother, fine.'

'And . . . and the children?'

'They are fine too.'

'I must get my luggage.'

'Yes, yes, of course.'

194

Fiona had expected much more luggage than her mother claimed, just two cases. She had taken twice as much with her she recalled. 'Would you like a cup of tea in the restaurant before we start out?' she said.

'No. No, thank you, dear. They give you a nice meal on the plane, and eating helps to shorten the journey. . . . Are you taking me to you . . . I mean is, have you made any arrangements about accommodation such as an hotel?'

'No, Mother; I didn't know what you intended to do. I thought you might like to come home with me first.'

'Yes. Yes, I would like that, Fiona. I . . . I have a lot to tell you.'

As they drove on to the main road from Newcastle Airport Mrs Vidler, who had been quiet for some time, said, 'It's nice to be back. I . . . I never thought I would say that, you know. Just to be back in England, it's a strange feeling.'

'Yes, yes, I suppose so.' Fiona could find nothing else to say. She felt at odds with this new mother, this different mother, this mother who seemed to be utterly devoid of aggression. She didn't know as yet how to handle her.

As they drove up the drive towards the house her mother now remarked, 'It's a lovely house.'

Then they were in the hall and she stood looking about her for a moment before turning to Fiona and saying, 'It's very beautiful. I . . . I never imagined it like this. Oh, hello! Mark.'

'Hello, Grandma.' Mark came up to her and dutifully kissed her on the cheek; and she smiled at him, saying, 'I can't believe it. You've grown so tall. And Willie!' She was now being kissed by Willie.

'Hello, Grandma,' he said.

'Hello, Willie. You too have grown. But then a lot happens in a year.'

Fiona, who was helping her off with her coat, noticed

that her mother had lost all her slimness. She'd had an almost sylph-like figure, but she had definitely thickened around the hips and waist; in fact, she appeared plump.

'Come into the sitting-room. . . .Mark, tell Nell we're back. She must be up in the nursery.' She turned to her mother. 'Nell's got a baby son,' she said. 'He's upstairs in the nursery with Angela.'

'Oh! Nell's got a baby. How nice for her.'

This indeed was not Mrs Vidler.

As they were about to enter the sitting-room Bill came running down the stairs; and they turned towards him, and he, now coming slowly up to them, said, 'Well, hello, Mother-in-law. You've got back then?'

'Yes, yes, I've got back.'

Fiona saw that he was nonplussed, which he certainly was; he was wondering where the old bitch was, the arrogant old bitch, the old bitch that hadn't a good word for him, ever.

'Well, come in and sit down. That was what you were goin' to do, wasn't it, both of you?' he said; and he marched before them into the room talking loudly, as much from embarrassment as from anything else. 'Nobody attends to this fire if I don't see to it. I'll get those three lazy young beggars on to that saw and get some logs cut up.'

They were just seated when Nell came into the room and she, remembering Mrs Vidler's manner towards her in the past, said politely, 'I hope you had a good journey, Mrs Vidler.'

'Yes. Yes, thank you. It was rather tiring, but when you think of it, it's very quick. Just a few hours between here and America. Yet such a vast distance really.' Her voice seemed to trail away on the last words. And now Nell said, 'I bet you could do with a cup of tea, real English tea.'

Mrs Vidler glanced at her daughter, then said, 'Yes; yes I could. Thank you.'

When Nell went out of the room there was silence among them for a moment. And then, to Fiona's and Bill's utter surprise they watched the scourge of their lives, and she had certainly been that, droop her head forward and quickly take a handkerchief from the sleeve of her dress and press it over her eyes.

'Oh! Mother. Mother.' Fiona was sitting on the couch beside her now, her arm around her shoulder. 'What is it?'

'I'm sorry, dear, I'm sorry. It's just that I . . . I never thought I'd . . . get home again. I never thought I'd be able to see you or . . . or any of the children. But' – she looked up at Bill now through her streaming eyes – 'I . . . I won't impose. I promise you, I won't impose ever again. I've still got the money for the house and . . . and I'll get a little place. In the meantime, I can go into a small hotel. I won't impose.'

'Be quiet! woman. What are you talkin' about imposin'? I don't know what's happened to you, but being me I'll tell you straight: it's somethin' in a way, that's done you good. As for imposin', by all means get a place of your own but in the meantime there's a room for you. That's what you want, isn't it, Fiona?'

Fiona stared up at him, her mouth slightly agape. 'Oh, yes, yes, Bill, definitely yes.'

'Aye, well, that's settled. Now, come on, tell us what happened and what's brought you back?'

Mrs Vidler now dried her eyes, took in a deep breath and, looking from one to the other, she began, 'Everything seemed marvellous at first. He had a very nice house, something like this' – she looked about her – 'beautifully furnished, and there was a swimming pool attached, and for the first week or two he couldn't do enough. He had proposed marriage or . . . well, suggested it strongly in his letters. But there was no mention of that when I got there but a lot of talk about my finances and about me putting

197

money into his estate business, which he told me was making small fortunes. When I told him I wasn't a rich woman, he laughed. You see I had been at this Hydro' – she bent her head again – 'stupidly to have this done' – she now dabbed her cheek with her forefinger – 'and that cost me a deal of money, more than I could really afford. And he went on that and the fact that I had a house in England and that I even had a daughter married to a' – she glanced at Bill – 'a prosperous builder. He kept asking when the money was coming through from the sale of the house. But perhaps you know that it was on the market six months before it was sold. Then one night I had been wined and dined by one of his so-called rich friends and from what was said I realised he thought I was a very wealthy woman but a bit cagey about what I was worth. And I suppose that started me thinking. Then when I got back, unexpectedly early, I found the man I thought of as my prospective husband, going through my things. He had actually opened a locked leather case I kept my papers in and also my bank book. Well' – she now swung her head in a desperate fashion – 'there was a dreadful scene. He said I'd hoodwinked him, not that he had hoodwinked me. And . . . and it turned out that this wonderful house of his had been rented just as it stood for three months, and that was almost up. He . . . he called me names. Dreadful. He walked out, took his things and went. That was the last I saw of him. There was a maid in the house and he had told her that I would pay her a month's wages in lieu of notice, and I told her I couldn't because I had very little money left until I got some sent from here. She was very kind to me. She . . . she told me that she had known all along he was a fake. And it turned out that he had been married and –' she swallowed deeply before she said, 'divorced three times. Fiona –' she now looked at her daughter and her lips trembled as she said, 'can you imagine how I felt? The humiliation, and to know that I'd been a stupid, a really stupid woman, a stupid . . . ageing woman.

198

I don't know what I would have done if it hadn't been for that girl, the maid. She knew the town and she got me into cheap lodgings.' She shook her head. 'And they were cheap lodgings.'

'But if that only covered three months, what have you been doin' all this time?' Bill demanded.

'Yes. Yes, Bill, what have I been doing all this time?'

It wasn't lost on Bill or Fiona that she had addressed him by his Christian name for the first time, which emphasised the change that had come over this woman. And when she repeated, 'You might well ask. Work is as difficult to get there as it is here, more so when you're British, and you have to have a work permit, even for a short time, oh that was difficult, so difficult, and they laugh at you the way you speak, even the way you walk. Anyway, I eventually ended up as an underpaid assistant nanny.'

'*Oh! Mother. You?*' She stopped here, and Mrs Vidler added, 'Yes, my dear, an assistant nanny to three dreadful children, spoilt, ruined, and even wicked in the things they did, not only to the other nanny and myself but to others in the household. And all the while I thought of my grandchildren. Yes, dear, my grandchildren. And yes, dear, for the first time I thought how they had been brought up. And I longed to be home, back in England. But I was so ashamed of myself, my stupidity . . . and vanity. If anyone in this world has been brought low, dear, it's been me.' She nodded at Fiona.

'You've been a damn fool.'

'Yes, yes, Bill, I've been a damn fool.'

'What I mean is,' said Bill, 'you should have wired. You could have had some money sent out to you until the house was sold.'

'I thought of that but I couldn't bring myself to.'

'Well, what brought you to it in the end then? Tell us that?'

'What brought me to it was that the nanny had had enough and I was left with those three dreadful children. And after three weeks, when I threatened to leave, the so-called mistress told me that she wouldn't give me a reference and I wouldn't be engaged by anyone in that town again. It was my business, she said, being a so-called English lady, that was her term, to improve her children's manners and what was more, to control their actions. It was then I went out and phoned you, dear.'

'What about the money for the house? Wasn't that sent on to you?'

'No. I told my bank manager not to send it on because I knew in my heart that I couldn't stay there forever. But I needed to pluck up the courage; and that awful woman, the mother of those three little devils, gave it to me. And I went out and phoned you. I would have got on a plane the next day but . . . but today was the nearest vacancy that was on the chartered flights. Oh, you don't know' – she now looked from one to the other – 'what it's like to be back. Oh' – she nodded her head now – 'the type of people there are in the world, moneyed people and those who are out to make it no matter what they do or how they do it, or who they hurt in the process. It's all money there. Without money you're nobody. It's true. You might think that wealth is badly divided here, but you've seen nothing until you go to America. Yet there are nice people there, like the maid. I don't know what I would have done without her. Then there was the nanny. We got on very well together, she and I, supporting each other, until she could stand no more. She was an American too and she was a generous girl, not like her employers. They were mean, narrow, except with food.' She nodded. 'They wasted food. And you know it's dreadful to admit, I . . . I who was always going on diets, I ate and ate. It was my only comfort, and this is proof of it.' She tapped her hips now.

'Aye, well, you can say it's been an experience. But now

200

that you're back you're welcome to stay until you get on your feet again an' find a suitable place. And I say the only sensible thing you've done is to leave the money for the house here. By the way, what did it go for?'

'Sixty-two thousand.'

'No!'

'Yes. It brought a good price; but then it was a very nice bungalow, as you know.'

'Well I can see how that bloke wanted to get his hands on that for his real estate or whatever.'

'Oh yes, he wanted to get his hands on it all right. That was the only thing he wanted. He kept pressing me to write to the agent. In fact, in the second month when nothing had happened he typed out a letter and got me to send it. It was from then I began to feel uneasy.'

'Ah, here's Nell with the tea. Hurry up, woman; you've had long enough to go to the plantation an' pick the leaves.'

'Hasn't he got a beautiful drawing-room manner?' Nell was speaking to Fiona now, and she answered, 'Yes; and I've always admired it, Nell. Such an example to others.'

'Is he talking yet?'

'What d'you mean, is he talking yet? Who?'

'Who but young Master Andrew.'

'Funny cuts, aren't you!'

Bill now turned to Mrs Vidler. 'It shouldn't surprise me,' he said, 'but her and Bert have bred a genius. He'll be writing symphonies at three or singin' them because he yells all the time. Be prepared, mother-in-law: you'll hear nothing but baby talk in this house from now on.'

Nell again addressed Fiona, saying, 'And who will lead the chorus?'

'Yes indeed, Nell, who will lead the chorus?'

And so it went on, cross-talk and light chipping to put the visitor at ease for what they were all witnessing was pride

201

having been brought low, and if anyone needed bolstering at this moment, it was this once arrogant bitchy mother, and mother-in-law, this once proud impossible woman.

3

It was a fortnight later when Bill helped Davey out of the car and into the house and sat him in the drawing-room in order to give him breath and strength to make the stairs. And just as the arrival of the child had altered their lives and the routine of the house, so did the arrival of Davey Love when he came into the house to die. They all knew, as he did, that he was dying; yet, years later, each individual was to look back to that time and see it as one of the most peaceful and happiest times that had reigned in that house.

The en suite bedroom overlooking the drive had a rose pink carpet with velvet curtains to match, these standing against French grey flock wallpaper that had a delicate browny pink stripe. The bed, a double one, had been placed with the head near the window and opposite on a small raised hearth stood the electric log fire that had graced Fiona's sitting room in the old house.

Altogether it was a beautiful room, and the first sight of it had brought tears to Davey's eyes. And when, on that first evening, he had said, 'What better place could God design for a man to die in,' Bill had exclaimed loudly, 'For the Lord's sake! Davey, stop talkin' like that,' only for Davey to come back at him and say quietly, 'Come here, boss. Sit down a minute.' And when Bill had obeyed him Davey said, 'Let's get this straight, boss, eh? Me time's runnin' out but me heart's overflowin' with gratitude. Will you believe me when I tell you, I'm happy? I've never been happier in me life. And that's honest to God, who I'll meet up with in a short time.' And then he had added on a laugh, 'It might be Saint Michael the Archangel, of course. Well, he's a tougher proposition, so I'm told. The situation'll be like everything else down here: when you get to the boss you've got a chance of gettin' a fair hearin'. It's them bods on the way up that have got opinions of themselves. They're the ones you can't get past. And don't I know it. So, boss, let's be happy, eh?'

And so it would seem that everyone in the house had taken their cue from the man who was now the centre of it; and none more so than Katie and, of all people, Susan Vidler. Both had taken on the post of part-time nurse.

Mrs Vidler, at odd times during the day, would sit with Davey, and it would appear that Katie couldn't get back quickly enough from school to take up her position near his bed and chat with him.

When he could no longer stagger to the bathroom, it was Sammy, Willie and Bill who took over the duties of seeing to his personal needs in that way. Bill made it his business to pop home every dinner-time, and the two boys came in from school just after four o'clock. If he needed attention before that, strangely again, it was Susan Vidler who saw to him. And there wasn't a day went by that the room didn't ring with laughter from one or another. One day in particular was when the priest came to visit him.

Father Hankin was a tall gaunt-looking man in his early thirties. He was known to be a man of wide views welcoming those of other denominations into conference. But on this day, sitting by the side of Davey's bed sipping a cup of tea, he looked from Fiona to Mrs Vidler, then to Davey before

204

he said, 'There's one thing I want to speak about and I suppose I'm going to affront your good friend here.' He now nodded towards Fiona. 'But it's about Sammy. Yes, yes, I know he attends his duties. He's a good boy in that way, but he's also attending the Protestant school – now isn't he? – and a private one at that.'

'Well, all I can say for that, Father, is thanks be to God.'

'Well, I can't sort of give you God's opinion of it meself, but mine is, that there's still good teaching in Saint Hilda's. The nuns are splendid teachers; three of them with university degrees, three of them mind!'

'Aye; and one of them, Father, with hands on her like bloody iron hammers. Pardon me, pardon me.' As Davey's head drooped, the priest said, 'Well, I agree with you: Sister Catherine has hands on her like bloody iron hammers, but she's got a lot of bloody hard nails to hit there.'

Davey had one arm tight round his waist trying to stifle his laughter; Fiona's mouth was wide, and although she had her hand over her mouth the sound of her laughter was loud; and although one would have expected Mrs Vidler to look askance and say, 'Dear! dear! dear! What language!' all she did was bite her upper lip to try and stop herself from roaring like the rest. The priest himself had his head back and his guffaws filled the room. Then, leaning towards Davey, he wiped his streaming eyes as he said, 'You see, you're not the only one, Davey, who's been to a special college. And I'd like to bet some of my brethren in the Cloth could beat you hollow.'

'I've no doubt 'bout that, Father,' replied Davey between gasps.

'Anyway, to come back to the serious subject of education,' the priest said: 'is it your wish that the boy continues where he is? Now think, think before you answer.'

'I have no time to think: I've no reason to think, Father, none at all, none at all. As long as it's possible I want him to stay at that school, then I'd hope he'd go on with Willie to Newcastle. There's a place called Dame Allan's there. . . .She must have been a very good woman to have a school named after her. Aye, she must. I've heard that's a good place for education. An' there's the Grammar school, too.'

'Well –' The priest once again leant towards Davey, saying now, 'If that's your wish, it's your wish. But mind, I'll tell you, if he doesn't keep up his duties I'll be after him, and I'll bring Sister Catherine with me an' all. Oh.' He turned now and looked from Mrs Vidler to Fiona and, his head bobbing, he said, 'I've got to admit it, between you and me, she'd make her way into the Vatican and scare the pants off the Pope, that one.'

Again the room rang with laughter.

Christmas was a happy affair. Most of the present opening and the festivities with the exception of the meals had taken place in the sick room. And it was only late on the Christmas night, when father and son were together for a short time, that Sammy, standing near the side of the bed, said, 'It's been a lovely day, hasn't it, Da?'

'Wonderful day, lad, wonderful day. You know somethin'? I've said it afore since I came into this house, but I'll say it again and especially for you – an' you've got to remember this – I've never been happier in me life. If heaven is any better than this I wonder why I'm goin'. They're wonderful folks you fell among, lad. And you know something else?' He leant forward, his eyes bright and moist. 'It was all through me teachin' you to swear.'

'Aw! Da.' Sammy pushed his father in the shoulder; then grinning, he said, 'But you're right. Aye, you're right. And I wasn't only swearin', was I? No, no. Four-letter 'uns, and they weren't spelt like our name, were they, Da?'

'No, they weren't, lad, they weren't. But it's funny how things happen, isn't it? So, I've done some good in the world after all, 'cos if you hadn't heard me you wouldn't have known half of 'em.'

'But you didn't use four-letter ones, Da.'

'No.' Davey considered a moment before admitting, 'No; except once or twice on me own outside the house I might have, but not in front of you. And I didn't want you to use them either. Yet around that quarter there were five-year-olds comin' out with 'em. They knew no better so it was understandable you pickin' them up. But' – he paused – 'this is a different life, lad, isn't it?'

'Yes, Da, it is a different life. That's why I always like to come here. I knew there was something I wanted but I didn't know what. But it was to live in a different way from around Bog's End.'

'Well, now, you're gettin' a good start, an' 'cos of it, God helpin' you, you'll grow up to be a good man. Another thing.' He now punched Sammy gently. 'Make people laugh. Play yersel' down, lad, you know what I mean, an' they'll laugh at you. That's the secret, play yersel' down except among your true friends. Aye, an' even those, 'cos if people think you haven't got much up top it makes them feel better, thinkin' they've got more. You know what I mean?'

'Aye. Da, I know what you mean.' And the boy, looking at this big gaunt man, realised for the first time that his da wasn't as thick as he made out to be, that he had never been as thick as he had always made out to be. It had been a sort of a game with him. His da, in a way, had been wise; but then he hadn't known that, not until now. And until now he hadn't realised how much he would miss him, at least not to the extent that he was going to.

He recalled that his da had made a pact with God to go to Mass every Sunday for a year if He did something for him. He wondered if he, too, were to make a pact with Him would it come off? If he said to Him, 'God, I'll become a priest if You make me da better.' But no; he knew it wouldn't

207

work for the simple reason he didn't want to become a priest. Another thing, it didn't do to make bargains with God. Look what had happened to his da.

'Come on, cheer up!' said Davey now, pushing his finger under the boy's chin. Then he added, 'I'm gona ask you to do somethin' for me. I know you're not one for the lasses, but Katie – she's a very unhappy lass is Katie. It's all because of what happened this time last year. So you could be nice to her, talk to her. I notice she doesn't talk much to the others.'

'She talks to you though, Da.'

'Aye. Yes, now that is funny, 'cos you know, she was a snooty piece was Katie. Oh aye, you she thought common; but I knew I was the mud in the bottom of the gut in Katie's opinion. That was when we first came on the scene. But she's a different girl now. She's been through trouble, love trouble, and, oh God in heaven! there's nothin' worse than that. Oh no. So, be kind like to her; don't argue with her or snap back at her.'

'I don't, Da.'

'No, but you're not very talkative I notice, not with her. With Willie or Mark it's twenty to the dozen, but with her. . . .'

'Well, she doesn't give you the chance, Da.'

'Well, it's up to you to make the chance. Just talk to her. She's like her granny, she's been brought low, 'cos if there ever was a change in a woman it's been in Mrs Vidler. Don't you think?'

'Aye, Da.'

' 'Tis an awful thing to bring people low, Sammy. When your ma walked out on us, I meself was brought low. Oh aye, I felt I wasn't a man; all me spunk was knocked out of me, 'specially' – he now pulled a face – 'when I saw what she picked in preference to meself. By! talk about the runt of the litter; it was a shame to wipe the wall with him.' He gave a sort of giggle now. 'And I did wipe the wall with that

208

poor fella. But why in the name of God! am I sayin' poor fella. He was a dirty bugger, now wasn't he?'

'Aye, Da, he was a dirty bugger.'

They laughed uproariously, and Sammy was on the point of saying, 'Stop it, Da! you'll die laughing,' but managed to check himself as he thought: He could at that. Aye, he could at that. Yet it wouldn't be a bad way for him to die. But oh dear Lord, he hoped it wouldn't be for weeks, and weeks, and weeks.

Bill found a bungalow for Mrs Vidler. It was on a small estate and it was only a five-minute drive from the house. She was very pleased with it, and for thirty-eight thousand it was well within her pocket and could be considered a bargain, for it was in good decorative repair and the previous owners were leaving the carpets and curtains, which again she found tasteful. The only thing now was to furnish it. She could have moved into it within a week. But on this particular night while sitting in the drawing-room having their coffee after the evening meal, she said to Bill, 'How long has he got . . . Davey?'

And Bill answered, 'I asked the same question of the doctor only yesterday. An' what he said was, he should have gone by now and he likely would have if he had been in hospital. He was kind enough to say we had kept him alive much longer than he himself expected. He was given three months at the most when he left the hospital but now here we are at the end of March and we can't hope that he'll go much longer. He said a week, two or three at the most. But before that happens he'll increase the dose so that he won't feel any pain.'

'I didn't tell you' – he was looking at Fiona now – 'but I found the youngster cryin' last night, and Willie cryin' with him. They were up in the bedroom. And I reassured Sammy again that this was his home now and for always. Then I had to get out else they would have had me at it. We're

209

either laughin' or cryin' in this house, there seems to be no happy medium.'

'Why I asked was,' put in Mrs Vidler now, 'if you'd mind if I stayed on until it's over. I was always fond of him, you know.' She looked slightly shamefaced now as she added, 'In the wrong way, I suppose; but nevertheless it was there.'

'You stay as long as you like, Mother-in-law. I can say now I've been pleased to have you.' Then leaning towards her, he said, 'Fancy me sayin' that, eh?' And she, bending towards him too, answered, 'And fancy me taking it. The next thing you know I'll be swearing back at you. That'll shake you.' As the laughter filled the room the door opened and Katie came in. She looked sad as she walked up to Fiona and, standing by her side, looked down at her, saying, 'He hasn't eaten his supper. And he asked if he could have a cup of coffee, black. He doesn't usually have it black. Can he have it?'

'Yes, yes, of course, dear. And I'll go up and see.'

'You'll sit where you are.' Bill put his hand out. 'Make a cup of coffee.' He looked at the tall young girl and she at him. 'You can make a cup of black coffee, can't you?'

'Yes; I can make a cup of black coffee.'

'Very well then. Go on, take it up to him.'

Oh dear, that always pained her. Fiona watched her daughter walk straight-backed out of the room. The way he spoke to her. Never unbent. She was lonely, and lost, and she herself couldn't get near her. . . .

Katie made the cup of black coffee and took it upstairs on a tray. And when she handed it to Davey, he said, 'Now why should I fancy a cup of black coffee? Eh, Katie?'

'I don't know.' She shook her head. 'You've never drunk black coffee before, not that I know of.'

'No; but I just suddenly thought that . . . well, milk was a bit plain. But why black coffee? Still, let me taste it.' He sipped at the cup, then said, 'Yes, it's nice. Refreshing. Not so cloyin' as milk, if you get what I mean.'

'Yes, I get what you mean.'

'Sit down aside me and have a bit of crack. Is everybody downstairs finished eatin'?'

'Yes. And we're all washed up. It was the boys' turn tonight.'

'How you gettin' on at school?'

'So-so.'

'Just so-so?'

'Yes; I . . . I don't seem able to concentrate.'

'Well, you used to. You came out top last year, they tell me, miles ahead of the rest. Gallopin' like an Irish cuddy over everybody in your class.'

She smiled at him now, saying, 'How do Irish cuddies gallop, Davey?'

'Aw, well, bein' Irish, they bring their back legs for'ard first, and havin' done that the front ones are bound to move: the back 'uns sort of kick the front 'uns for'ard. You see what I mean?'

'Well, going on that symbolism, those at the back of the class will come forward and beat those at the front.'

He thought a moment before he said, 'Aye, you're right, you're right there. But as I said, they were Irish cuddies.'

'I wish I had been born Irish.'

'In the name of God! why? I ask you, why?'

'So that I could laugh easily. You laugh easily. You make people laugh easily. All Irish people do that.'

'Oh, no, begod! you're wrong there. Not all Irish folk make people laugh. Some of 'em make people angry an' bitter. Oh, don't get it into your head that all Irish folk are funny. Like every other people, there's some an' some, an' some of the same, if you follow what I mean, are stinkers, although I say it meself an' about me own folk. In any case, most of 'em don't just want to make people laugh. Oh, no, lass, all Irish people don't laugh. But I'll tell you somethin'. You should laugh more.'

211

'I've nothing to laugh about except when I'm with you. You make me laugh.'

'You think your da's still vexed with you, don't you?'

'I don't think, I'm sure. He dislikes me now. He doesn't hate me but he dislikes me.'

'Nonsense.'

'It isn't, Davey. Anyway, he's not my real father so it will be quite easy to dislike me. If he had been my real father he would have forgiven me a long time ago for what I did.'

'Did you ever go to him an' tell him you were sorry for what you did?'

'No. No, I couldn't because for some time after I wasn't sorry. I was in a sort of state I suppose. Older people would call it a stupid state, a phase. But I still hated that girl, the woman. He's living with her now, you know.'

'Aye, I know. And he deserves some happiness. An' she was a nice enough miss.'

'Yes. You danced with her and she laughed a lot with you.'

'Aye, she did. An' what's the harm in that?'

'There was no harm as long as it was you, but when it was with him it changed everything.'

'And how d'you feel about him now?'

She looked away from the bed and towards the log fire and its flickering flames, and she said, 'It's funny, odd, I feel nothing. I wonder why I was so stupid. I'll never be that stupid again. Not over anybody.'

'Aw, don't say that. You will one day 'cos you're goin' to grow into a beautiful woman. With that hair an' those eyes, you'll have 'em runnin' after you like that Irish cuddy.'

'Well, it won't matter to me, Davey, if they run after me because I don't think I'll ever like anybody again, not in the way that I liked him. And the awful thing is to know it was no use. And if a feeling like that can die anything can die.'

'That's 'cos you're young, dear. You're just fifteen years

212

old. As you say, you were in a phase. Well, you'll still be in a phase for some time yet.'

'I'm not just fifteen, Davey, not inside I'm not; I feel old, well, old in a way because I've experienced something that I shouldn't have experienced for a long, long time. No one of fourteen should have a feeling that makes them feel ferocious. I felt ferocious and I knew I wasn't fourteen inside.'

Davey sighed now as they stared at each other, and he said, 'What d'you intend to be, dear?'

She put her head on one side, then said, 'I've thought about that of late, more so since you came to live with us. And I think I'd like to be a nurse.'

'That's good. That's good. But it's no easy job. I'm amazed at what nurses had to do when I was in hospital. They worked like Trojans.'

'I wouldn't mind the work, but being a nurse you'd be sort of able to disperse yourself or dispense yourself.'

'What d'you mean, disperse or dispense yourself?'

'Well, I suppose I mean spread yourself around, not put all your feelings or affections on one person.'

'Aw, lass, that's a daft idea. If that's all you're goin' in for nursin' for, I'd give it up now. Yes, I would. Honest to God, I'd give it up now. Spreadin' yourself around. Dear me! Dear me! An' when that fella on the white horse comes ridin' by, you'd have nothin' to give to him, 'cos you'd be skin and bone.'

'Oh, Davey, you are funny.'

'No, I'm not in this case, Katie, I'm not funny.' His face looked serious as did his voice sound, 'Don't think of spreadin' yourself around hinny, in any way. Keep yourself, what you call, intact. Remember that word, intact, until the fella who's worthy of you comes along. He might come as a surprise or on t'other hand he might be somebody you've known for years, an' you'll look at him as if you're seein' him for the first time. It happens with a man an' all

213

you know. It happened to meself, it did that. I spread meself around an' all, in a way, until I'd nothin' to give to me wife. And what does she do? She walked out on me. But you know all that, don't you?'

He laid his head back on the pillow and, moving his eyes around the room as far as he could see, he said, ''Tis a beautiful room this, Katie, a beautiful room. An' your mother's a beautiful woman, an' your dad is a fine man, one of the best that walks the earth. Loud-mouthed, mind.' He lifted his head slightly and grinned at her now. 'Oh, aye, loud-mouthed, but behind his bellowing he's a carin' man. And he cares for you.' He turned his head now and looked at her. 'He cares for you deeply. And there'll come a time when you'll just need to put your hand out and he'll be there to hold it.'

After a moment of silence she said, 'Your coffee's nearly cold. You didn't like it?'

'Oh, yes, I did, I mean I do. Look, I'll drink it all up.'

'You don't have to.'

'Don't I now?'

'No. It was just a passing fancy, wasn't it?'

'Aye, perhaps. I don't know what made me ask for black coffee, 'cos I've never understood the blokes that like it, I mean that like drinkin' it after a meal. Yet there I go, askin' for black coffee. It's fancies I'm gettin' in me old age.'

'You're tired. Don't talk any more.'

'You're an understandin' girl, Katie, you're an understandin' girl. Yes, yes, I'm tired. By the way, what's the day?'

'It's Friday.'

'And we're in March. I never thought, well to tell you the truth, I never thought to see March. It's the kindness that's kept me here.'

She now watched his lips press tightly together and his lids screw up pressing his eyes back into the sockets. And

214

his voice a whisper as he said, 'Will you send your da to me, Katie?'

'Oh, yes, yes.' She jumped up from the chair and ran from the room, and this time she burst into the drawing-room, saying, 'He's bad! He's asking for you.' She was nodding at Bill and Sammy. 'I think he's in pain.'

Bill and Sammy rushed from the room now, followed by Fiona, and Katie was left with her grandmother. And when the older woman moved towards her, Katie threw herself into her arms, and Susan Vidler, said, 'Don't cry, Katie. Don't cry for him. He's had much longer than any of us thought.'

'I'm so unhappy, Gran. In all ways, I'm so unhappy.'

'I know you are, dear, and I know why. We've both been silly people, but mainly for the same reason. Strange that, isn't it? An old woman and a young girl making fools of ourselves. But it's all in the past. There now, there now. It'll all come right because, as Davey himself would say, you've done your penance and I've done mine.'

4

Three weeks later when they buried Davey, it was a bright April day, with the daffodils filling the vases on the graves and the green verge along the path being full of them. Fifty of Bill's men were present. One person was noticeable by her absence and that was Davey's mother. She was in hospital having a hip operation. Rupert was also present but Miss Isherwood, now known as Mrs Meredith, was not with him. Father Hankin who had said Mass over the coffin in the Catholic church was now saying the prayers for the dead. Sammy stood by the graveside and on each side of him stood Fiona and Bill, and next to Bill was Willie, and standing beside him was Mark. Slightly behind them were Mrs Vidler and Katie. Nell was not present. She had voted to stay behind to see to the children. She had confessed to Fiona she abhorred funerals.

When the first clod of earth hit the coffin Fiona felt Sammy shudder and as she went to put her hand on his shoulder she noticed Bill's arm come round it. Then one after the other the people dispersed until there was only the family left. And then they too moved away.

They were nearing the chapel in front of which all the wreaths and flowers were displayed. And as they paused to

216

look at them a man, who was passing, stopped, and Fiona said, 'Hello, Rupert. It was nice of you to come.'

'Hello, Fiona.' He paused, then added, 'I'm sorry he's gone. I liked him. But who didn't when they got to know him.' He turned his eyes to the side now, and there standing not two feet away from her mother was Katie. He stared at her for a moment and she at him, and then he said, 'Hello, Katie.' And another moment passed before she answered simply, 'Hello.'

Bill now turned from viewing a large wreath that his men had sent and, stepping up to them, he said, 'Hello there, Rupert. He was well represented, wasn't he?'

'He was indeed, Bill.'

Bill gave a swift glance towards Katie, but her face was utterly blank.

'Would . . . would you like to come back for a drink, Rupert?' Fiona said.

'Thank you, but . . . but I've got to get back to work –' He nodded towards Bill, a half smile on his face now, then added, 'or he'll be asking what does he pay me for. But I'd like to pop in sometime if I may.'

'You'll be very welcome at any time.'

'I'll do that then. I'll have a word now with Sammy. Be seeing you then.' He nodded from one to the other, including Katie, then turned to where Sammy and Willie were looking at the wreaths. Bill, his voice low now, yet in a way light, said, 'Well, let's get home,' and turned to Fiona, saying, 'You take the womenfolk and I'll take the men, the same as when we came.'

And they walked out of the cemetery now and got into the cars, and fifteen minutes later they were getting out of the cars again and filing into the house.

It was as they stood in the hall, taking their coats off, that Fiona noticed that Katie was standing apart. She hadn't taken off her coat. She was standing stiffly staring towards Bill, and Fiona, in the act of taking Bill's coat from him,

217

made a motion with her head that caused him to turn round; and as he did so and looked at Katie standing, her head up, her mouth open, the tears came streaming down her face and, on a gasp, she cried, 'I'm sorry, Dad. Oh! I'm sorry. I'm sorry. I am.'

Quickly he went and put his arms about her and held her close, saying, 'There! there! So am I, lass. So am I. Come on now, it's all over. Come on into the drawing-room and sit down.'

Slowly she drew herself away from him. 'I'll . . . I'll, go upstairs for a minute,' she said. 'I'll be down directly. I'll just . . . just tidy up.' Then bending abruptly forward, she kissed him and ran from him up the stairs. And he, turning, first looked at Fiona, then at his mother-in-law, and said quietly, 'Back to normal. Thank God for it. Back to normal.' Then glancing towards the passage from where Bert had appeared carrying his son, followed by Nell holding Angela by one hand and Mamie by the other, Bill nodded, saying, 'Family en masse.' Then addressing Bert pointedly, he said, 'You beat me to it. Couldn't get home quick enough.'

Bert now looked about him, saying, 'Where's Sammy?'

It was Willie who answered, 'He's just gone upstairs. He'll be down in a minute.'

Sammy was coming out of the bathroom when he saw Katie running into her room; and he stood on the landing for a moment wiping his eyes; then walking slowly up to her door he knocked, and after what could have been a full minute she opened it. And she showed her surprise at seeing him standing there, but she said, 'You want to see me, Sammy?'

'Aye.' He went past her and stood in the room and, looking up at her, because she was still taller than him, he said, 'You liked me da, didn't you?'

'Yes. Yes, I was very fond of him . . . very. We . . . I mean, I could talk to him. We talked a lot.'

218

'Aye, I know you did. And him and me talked a lot an' all, and about you.'

'About me?' She dug her fingers into her chest; and he said, 'Aye. And you know what?' He gave a wan smile now, 'He told me I had to talk to you.'

'He told you that! Why?'

'I don't know except that you weren't talkin' to anybody these days, only to him. And he must have thought when he was gone you still wouldn't talk to anybody, and I'd be better than nothing. But then I don't suppose you will need me to talk to you now.'

'But I will, Sammy. Yes, I will.' Her voice was urgent now, her expression eager. 'You know, you're very like your da. You see, I'm even getting to talk like you.'

'Eeh! you'd better not do that' – their smiles mingled – 'else I'll get me head in me hands and me brains to play with.'

Her smile widened now as she said, 'That's exactly what your father would have said.'

His face became straight; then his lips trembled for a moment before he said, 'I mean to make something of meself 'cos that would have pleased him. But I'll have to live a long time to repay everybody in this house for what they've done for me.'

Her smile became a grin now as she said, 'Well, you can start by talking to me and pay it off at so much an hour.'

'Aye, that's an idea.'

They stared at each other in silence now, and when he slowly put his hand out she took it, and when he said, 'I feel sort of lost,' she said quietly, 'I know the feeling, but it'll pass.'

'I'm gona miss me da. And you know something? He was a wise man and I never knew it until a short while ago.'

'Well, I've got one over on you there because I found that out soon after he came into the house.'

'You did?'

'Yes.'

Again they looked at each other in silence, then he said, 'We'd better be getting down,' and they turned together and went out of the room, and only became conscious that they were still holding hands when they neared the stairhead.

As their hands dropped to their sides they laughed sheepishly, and it was Katie who said, 'That would have given them something to get their teeth into, wouldn't it?' And when he answered, 'By! aye, it would that, enough to get me thrown out,' they again laughed before walking side by side like two people who knew they had discovered something in each other.